The sound wasn't coming from the attic. It was at her bedroom door—a light tapping.

"Is that you, Mrs. Bellinger?" Gail called out.

She left her bed, went to the door and un-latched it, expecting the housekeeper to open the door from the other side. When nothing happened, Gail decided to turn the knob herself. She opened the door.

A figure in a bloody nightgown was on the other side—a standing corpse. Then red-smeared sleeves were lifted slowly and dead-white hands were extended toward Gail, dangling limply from the deeply gashed wrists.

"Come with me," the ghostly figure said.

THE THING AT THE DOOR
was originally published by Random House, Inc.

The Thing at the Door

Henry Slesar

PUBLISHED BY POCKET BOOKS NEW YORK

THE THING AT THE DOOR

Random House edition published 1974

POCKET BOOK edition published April, 1976

This POCKET BOOK edition includes every word contained in
the original, higher-priced edition. It is printed from brand-
new plates made from completely reset, clear, easy-to-read type.
POCKET BOOK editions are published by
POCKET BOOKS,
a division of Simon & Schuster, Inc.,
A GULF+WESTERN COMPANY
630 Fifth Avenue,
New York, N.Y. 10020.
Trademarks registered in the United States
and other countries.

Standard Book Number: 671-80427-8.
Library of Congress Catalog Card Number: 74-8225.

Printed in the U.S.A.

To Jan

The Thing at the Door

March 12, 1955

Dying smelled of medicine and furniture wax. The Gold Dust Twins had applied the latter all over the bureaus, cabinets, and stair railings of the Gunnerson house at the direction of Mrs. Bellinger, who thought the servants needed busywork to take their minds off the dwindling of life in the upstairs bedroom. Gail Gunnerson was going to feel an inexplicable sadness at the smell of polished wood for the rest of her life. She didn't know that yet; on March 12, 1955, she was only six years old. Her small hand slid smoothly on the polished bannister as she ascended to the second floor, tiptoing in her patent-leather shoes as if the heavy carpeting didn't mute the sound of her small footsteps.

At the top of the stairs she heard the click of a latch, and realizing that someone was emerging from her mother's bedroom, she did what fear commanded. She ran. There was a castle with a single imposing tower at the end of the hallway, a place of sanctuary. Others, older, more literal, called it a grandfather clock. Gail ducked behind it (more smell of wax, lemmony and stale, like a faded gardenia) and heard her uncle's voice, a reverberating male sound that made the clock's delicate springs quiver: "What time did the man say he would be here?"

"Within the hour, sir." Mrs. Bellinger.

"I wish he'd hurry. I want to catch the nine o'clock flight. Have you seen the girl?"

"No, sir."

"What about my son?"

"Downstairs, Mr. Swann."

"Piers!" He exploded the word over the stair railing like a depth bomb. Almost at once, Gail heard the boy's piping response from below. Then her uncle: "Have you seen your cousin?"

"No."

"Find her. Tell her to come to the bedroom."

"Gee, Pop, I don't know where she is."

"Look for her. Tell her, too, it's her last chance to see her mother—before the undertaker comes."

The word meant nothing and implied too much. Gail crouched into a small package beside the sheltering wall of the clock. She heard Piers calling her, heard him opening doors up and down the long hallway, slamming them irreverently, being fourteen years old and unimpressed by the death of strangers.

"Gail! Hey, where are you?"

She tried to remember the invisibility formula in the last book her mother had read to her. But memory failed, and Piers succeeded. "What are you doing there?" She whimpered a wordless reply. "What's the matter with you? My father says to come to the bedroom." She shrank from his outstretched hand. "Come on! Don't you want to see your mother?"

"No!"

"It's your last chance. They're going to take her away." There was enough toneless malice in his words to make her tears start flowing. She slapped at his hand and cried out: "I won't go!"

His hand on her arm. "You dumb kid! You *got* to see her, you're *supposed* to!"

"I won't, I won't!"

Pulling and tugging.

"Let go of me, Piers, let go! I don't want to see her. I won't go in there—I won't!"

The doorbell was ringing below, postponing the personal conflict. The Twins had left an hour earlier in a frenzy of sobs, so Mrs. Bellinger had to answer it herself. Piers seemed anxious to see the visitor, so he released Gail's arm and went to the stairwell. She heard him suck in his breath with an inside-out whistle that made curiosity overcome apprehension. She joined him at the railing and looked down.

There were three men in the doorway, two of them in identical jackets that gave them an authority somewhere between medical and military. The third man was more impressive. He was so tall that when he swept off the black felt hat the crown of it slapped the top of the door frame. His suit was black, too. Gail knew the color was associated with mourning, but somehow she realized that the sentiment was impersonal.

"The undertaker," Piers whispered.

Then they were coming up the stairs, and now Gail saw that one of them carried a device of wooden poles and canvas, but its significance didn't concern her; she was too riveted by the face of the man at the head of the solemn procession. In her six years she had been spared the sight of true ugliness; she saw it now, an ugliness heightened by an expression of grim, lugubrious purpose. And then, as they passed and entered her mother's bedroom, Piers compounded her dread by saying: "He's come for your mother. You're too late to see her now; he's going to take her away. He's going to take her away and put her in a wooden box."

She stared at her cousin, chilled by his flat, unteasing voice.

"It's true," Piers said. "That's what an undertaker

does. He puts you in a box. He puts the box under the ground and buries you!"

The three were coming out, with *her*. A sheet covered the body, from the crown of wheat-brown hair to the painted toenails, and Gail knew that everything Piers had said was cruel truth, that her mother's death was being followed by an ever greater horror, and it was time to let the screams come . . .

Tears salted the milk Mrs. Bellinger gave her. Gail had never been allowed the privilege of milk and cookies in her own bed, but this was a night of privilege. She said, "Are they gone? Is everybody gone?"

"Everybody, honey. Your Uncle Swann and your cousin Piers are on their way home . . . they're sorry they can't stay for the funeral tomorrow, but your uncle's got some very important business in London. You know where London is, honey, remember the pictures? The big clock I showed you, the clock named Ben?" Gail didn't respond. Mrs. Bellinger sought another distraction. She picked up the mechanical ballerina on the night table and wound it. "Now you go right to sleep, honey. I've got things to do downstairs, but I'll come upstairs when I'm finished and spend the night with you. All right?"

The ballerina turned slowly on her circular base. When the melody was more audible than Gail's sniffles, the housekeeper set it down, kissed the child's forehead, and went out of the room.

A few minutes later the ballerina tired of her dance, and the music slowed and ended, and Gail was asleep.

Before the time of dreaming she woke again.

She saw the ballerina first, frozen in an entrechat. She remembered death.

The porcelain body of the dancer was waxy-pale in the moonlight.

Death, the visitor.

She caught a sob in her throat and clutched at the covers for the warm brown fur of the Pooh Bear who shared her pillow. She held him close and thought of death.

Death, the incredible.

Then the knob creaked, metal grating metal, and Gail looked up, toward the light, toward a new shape of darkness.

The door was opening.

One

A man was following her.

When she first became aware of his synchronized footsteps, she made a mental check list of everything she should have carried, but didn't. One container of Mace. One police whistle. One hatpin. Then she caught a glimpse of the characteristic buckle of his Gucci shoes, and decided that the motive was lust, not loot.

It was the portfolio, of course; the flat black package under her arm. It wouldn't have been the first time a man had mistaken it for a model's accouterment, and some men had dull, crafty ideas about fashion models. For that matter, she could have been just what the portfolio implied; it could have contained composites advertising the golden profusion of her hair, the astonishing brown-velvet darkness of her eyes. But it didn't. Surprise, surprise, mister. Look what's inside. Different kinds of models. Fat ladies. Drawings of hairy women. Some of them dissected by her charcoal: a corpulent arm here, a leg there, a hand tilted in what was supposed to be a gracious Dürer-like gesture. If she could draw a hand, that is; why were hands so impossible to draw? Why couldn't people be all eyes and mouths and noses? She was very good on noses.

She crossed the street, and he crossed with her. She

crossed it again, in still another test, and he passed it, or failed it, depending on your point of view. She was too tired to become angered; what she felt was weary exasperation. Wasn't morning bad enough without this? Every morning was a punishment for her, since every preceding night was a trial. Last night had been one of the worst; she hadn't slept more than an hour or two. Her nightmares had ridden through her brain in brief, frenetic gallops.

When she was within sight of the Art League's gray stone doorway, she felt safe enough to slow down and even come to a complete halt, forcing her tracker to either pass on the left or make his move. He did neither. He simply stopped, pretended rapt interest in the Art League's showcase window. She saw his reflection blended against the fiery acrylics of Moses Liebling's last painting. He was good-looking. At least his reflection was. Not even-featured, but nice. Thin, not very broad-shouldered. Good hands, impossible to draw. But she was sure she could do that nose.

When she ducked into the doorway, he seemed surprised. She wondered if the truth had suddenly dawned on him; that he wasn't chasing the Girl from *Vogue* after all; he was only after a poor, starving artist. She made a face when the phrase entered her mind. Gail didn't fit any one of those three descriptions.

Mr. Liebling was moseying when she walked into the classroom. That was the word he used to describe his technique. He shuffled around the room, crowding his students, leaning his whiskery chin on their shoulders as they tried to sketch the live model in the center of the floor, commenting, grunting, complaining, rarely praising; in the three months of her study, Gail had heard only one kind word from his crinkled lips.

"Nice," he had said, and she still had no idea whether he was referring to her sketch or her bustline, since he was looking at both at the same time. Mr. Liebling, while routinely ignoring the nude models in his classroom, had an eye for the clothed female students.

Gail managed to avoid catching that eye as she entered and went to set herself up at her customary place, beside the easel of Helen Malmquist. Her friend made a clownish mouth and said: "Well, what's the excuse this time?"

"A man followed me here."

"So what else is new?"

"I mean really followed me. From my apartment all the way to the Art League. Seven blocks—can you imagine?"

"Did you get a look at him?"

"Only for a second."

"A creep?"

"No," Gail said. "He was youngish, good-looking."

"Then stop complaining. You should see what follows *me*."

Gail ignored the self-deprecation. There was nothing wrong with Helen's looks; her coloring was almost a negative of Gail's. Dark hair, light-blue eyes, a mouth too wide to allow the rest of her face to be called beautiful, but a traffic-stopping figure. At the moment, it stopped Moses Liebling, who put his chin against her right shoulder and squinted at her drawing. What there was of it. Helen never seemed to get further than a thin, shadowy contour which only vaguely resembled the subject. Sometimes Gail wondered if their friendship hadn't been born for that very reason; Helen was so inept that Gail's own renderings looked positively professional.

The instructor was shaking his head and making clucking noises. "You know what your trouble is, darling? You think too much. You have to stop all the thinking. You have to let your hand do the thinking. Big, bold strokes!"

He snatched the charcoal stick from her hand and used big, bold strokes to outline the model's figure; the heavy limbs appeared magically on the paper, the angle of elbow on plump thigh, even something of her dour expression. It turned out better than he expected, so he smiled good-naturedly and handed her back the charcoal.

"It's only a sheet of paper, darling," he said. "Don't be afraid of it."

He winked at Gail and moved on to the next student. Helen looked speculatively at her drawing pad, and then decided to add a finishing touch. She signed the drawing.

"What are you doing?" Gail asked.

Helen ripped off the page and rolled it up. "I'll show my old man I can draw!"

They brought a sandwich lunch to the park and Helen said: "Well? And how about *last* night?"

Gail shook her head. "No different. Quit asking me about that every day, Helen, you know I always give you the same answer. I'm just one of those people who don't sleep well."

"Then how do you do it? I mean, how does a girl who never gets her beauty sleep look so damned beautiful?"

"Eat your baloney."

"It's liverwurst . . . Gail, what about this doctor you went to see? Yost?"

"He gave me exactly the same prescription the last one gave me. I told him it wouldn't work. Oh, not that I wouldn't fall asleep, that phenobarb stuff hits me like a sledge hammer. But then I wake up in the middle of the night, as if I'd just heard a cannon shot, and my heart is beating a thousand times a minute. And then I'm a wreck the next day, a complete wreck. No, it isn't any kind of an answer, Helen; it never has been."

"And last night?"

"I didn't take anything. I just couldn't. I wanted to feel human today."

"And do you?"

"No."

"So you didn't sleep."

"I fell asleep," Gail said. "I never have much trouble doing that. But then . . ."

"Those dreams again, right?"

"You know something? Conversations about my health are about as interesting as—liverwurst sandwiches. How do you eat those things, anyway?"

"I need iron," Helen said, munching blankly, deep in thought. Gail respected the reverie and sipped quietly from the pint container of milk. Then Helen looked at her with a solemnity new to her face and said: "Honey, do you mind if I say something personal?"

"Go ahead."

"I've got a big mouth, anybody can see that, and sometimes I think that gives me the privilege of saying things. You shut me up if you think I'm out of line, but—well, you remind me of myself."

"In what way?"

"Oh, don't worry, I won't give you a case history. Talk about liverwurst—a couple of years ago I was nothing more then a pile of chopmeat. I mean, I had the worst case of screaming meemies you ever saw."

"*You* did?" By "you," of course, Gail was defining her happy-go-lucky nature.

"Every record has two sides. You're looking at the flip side." She crumbled up the remnants of her sandwich and stuffed them into the paper bag. "I'll tell you how bad it got," Helen said. "One night I went into the bathroom, got out a razor blade, and cut my wrists."

She unbuttoned the long-cuffed blouse, and Gail realized that she never wore anything but wrist-concealing clothes. The scars were thin, white, and long.

"Big, bold strokes," Helen said.

Gail was speechless.

"As you might have gathered," Helen said. "I did a lousy job. Naturally, they stuck me into a psychiatric ward; there was nobody around to cover up for me. When I came out, they put me under the care of a psychiatrist. A young one, fresh out of school, still wet behind the diploma. His name was Dr. Vanner. God bless every hair in his beard."

"He helped you?"

"He saved my life. I mean that absolutely literally."

"Do you still see him?"

"Only once a month. Just to keep the corners glued down." She smiled. "Vanner's a lot more expensive than he used to be. Office on Park Avenue. Real leather couch. When I knew him, he just put two kitchen chairs togather." She put her hand over Gail's, remembered the wrist marks, and buttoned her shirt carefully. "Honey, what I'm asking you is—have you ever seen someone like that?"

Gail hesitated before saying: "I didn't see any. But they saw *me*. They came to my house by the carload. And then there was a time when— Look, Helen, if all this is leading to 'Have I got a doctor for you,' please—forget it. I couldn't face that sort of thing again, honestly I couldn't."

"Okay, okay, it was just a friendly suggestion." She squeezed the paper bag into a smaller package and looped it toward the wire basket, missed. "I can't make points, can I?" She smiled. "You won't see my doctor, you won't even meet my friends. Or have you changed your mind about tonight?"

Gail lowered her eyes, and Helen sighed. "What kind of cocamamie friends are we? You don't know anybody I know, and the same goes for me."

"I'm sorry, Helen, honest I am—"

"Change your mind, Gail, why don't you? It'll be a gas. After you meet some of my friends, you'll think *you're* normal."

"The truth is, I'm just not much fun at parties. I get a terrible isolated feeling, and everybody around me feels it. I'm like an open refrigerator door . . ."

"Who knows?" Helen grinned widely, her mouth clownish again. "You might meet some guy who has the defrosting instructions."

Gail didn't reply.

On her way home she thought about Helen's remark. It was true, of course. She had never been to Helen's home, or invited Helen to hers. Suddenly she realized that she was ashamed of being rich. The curious discovery so absorbed her that she wouldn't have been aware of anything happening around her, certainly not of being followed again. As it happened, she was. By a pair of Gucci loafers.

Mrs. Bellinger was slapping flatfootedly around the kitchen. When she heard the front door slam, she removed the carpet slippers with the hand-cut bunion holes and groaned her way into a normal pair of shoes. She hated Gail to see signs of decay in her—not that her feet hadn't always been a problem. It was only after Gail's mother's death, only when Gail herself was in *that* place (Mrs. Bellinger never thought of the Mead Clinic as anything but *that* place) that Mrs. Bellinger had entered the hospital and allowed the surgeon to strip down the bulging veins in both legs. But even the phlebectomy hadn't helped her poor feet, twin homes for every wandering corn, callus, and bunion in the vicinity.

She came into the living room and said: "Gail, honey?"

But Gail had breezed through the room too quickly. She was already on the second floor and heading for her bedroom. The housekeeper-cum-mama called out to her again, unheard; she didn't venture the stairs. Mrs. Bellinger could hardly remember when she had climbed those stairs last. Of course, the other servants took care of the upper reaches of the house; her province was the kitchen. The Gold Dust Twins had long returned down South, but two others had taken their place. Three servants for one resident seemed exorbitant to some people, but Mrs. Bellinger knew it was the *house* that needed the domestic help, not Gail Gunnerson. And from Mrs. Bellinger, she needed more than housekeeping; she needed love and caring. The housekeeper believed this more firmly than she believed in God, and Mrs. Bellinger went to church even on weekdays.

She returned to the kitchen and decided to buzz the intercom in Gail's room. The device had been wired up when she was still an infant; her father had done the job on his last furlough before returning to South Korea and the shell fragment that was waiting to kill him.

"You all right, Gail?"

"Yes, Emma, I'm all right. Just tired out as usual. I thought I'd try a nap before dinner."

"Think you'll sleep okay tonight if you do?"

"I'm sure I *won't* sleep tonight. I'm sure I won't even nap well. But I'm going to try anyway."

"Honey, that man from the police called today. I can never remember his name."

"Lieutenant Baldridge."

"That's it. He said that there wasn't anything he could do about that patrol car business; there was no way they could change the routes."

"I thought that's what he'd say."

"He said the best thing we could do is change all the locks. He said maybe we ought to get a guard dog, whatever that is."

"Maybe a gorilla would be better than a dog. Do you suppose Hertz rents gorillas, Emma?"

"You sound awful sleepy, honey."

"I am," Gail said. "I don't know if I'll be able to get my clothes off in time. But I don't want to sleep straight through, Emma, that would be a disaster. So buzz me at seven-thirty, all right?"

"I made shrimp Marengo for dinner."

"Seven-thirty, Emma, okay?"

"All right," the housekeeper sighed. Then she hung up the phone and changed her shoes gratefully. She was glad she had them on an hour later when she heard the strange noises in the intercom speaker. Obviously Gail had been too groggy to switch off the instrument because now Mrs. Bellinger heard the high-pitched hysterical series of half-screams and half-sobs from the upstairs bedroom, and she said, "Dear God!" and forced her aching feet toward the stairs. She knew it was only another dream, another bad one, weren't they all? But she had never heard the sounds transmitted below, and they conveyed something both heartbreaking and frightening about Gail Gunnerson's nightmares. Because the sounds she made were the cries of a small and terrified six-year-old.

Two

"I have a feeling that my beard fascinates you," Dr. Vanner said.

"That's funny," Gail said coldly. "I had the same thought about you. The way you keep tugging at it."

He laughed, exposing good, strong white teeth amid the underbrush, and gave the point of his beard a slight upward tilt with his hand. "You know, you're right. But the reason is a bit oblique. I grew the beard when I left college, more than ten years ago. Believe it or not, a beard was an oddity ten years ago. Now, of course, it's no longer very remarkable."

"Except on old men," Gail said.

"Yes." Vanner chuckled. "That's the switch."

"Is that why you grew it originally? To look older?"

"Something like that. Inspire confidence in the patients. Or maybe just to venerate the memory of my idol, Sigmund You-Know-Who. Or maybe simply to make people think I was his reincarnation. I'll have to analyze that someday."

"Do you think you can afford your fees?"

Vanner's laugh came less easily. "Well. Here we are discussing the doctor, not the patient."

"I didn't say I was a patient. I just want to *talk* about this."

"All right, then let's talk. But it would help me to

know a little more than just your name, rank, and social security number . . ."

"Tell me what you want to know."

"Suppose I tell you what I already know—from your friend Miss Malmquist."

"Does she talk about me?"

"Only when she isn't talking about herself, her father, her cat, or her boyfriends. In that customary order, too."

"What did she tell you?"

"That you're an orphan. That your father died shortly after your birth, your mother when you were six. That you don't sleep well. That you have bad dreams. That you've seen other men with beards. Presumably with the same sort of diplomas on their walls."

"None of them had beards. And they were all much older."

"Does my age trouble you? Do you think I won't be able to help you solve your problem because I'm not mature enough, wise enough?"

"Are you?" she said, surprising herself.

"Do you have to be convinced?" Vanner said. "Miss Malmquist says she gave me quite a testimonial. If that isn't sufficient—well, maybe you need some demonstration of my powers."

"Such as?"

"Sherlock Holmes stuff. You know, Conan Doyle was a sort of psychoanalyst himself. His use of the inferential technique, the thing we mistakenly call 'deduction.' Learning facts about people without their explicit statement."

"Is there something you know about me? Just from the way I'm sitting here, talking to you? Body language?"

He chuckled. "Sorry, I don't speak it. Although if I did, I'd look at *your* body and say: 'Oh, boy.'"

Gail flushed, her skin violently pink in contrast to her blond hair. Vanner regarded the effect with interest and asked: "Does that statement bother you? Do you object to personal references, anatomic references?"

"If you think I've come here because of some sexual hang-up, Doctor—"

"I wasn't implying a thing." He leaned back and adopted a graver tone. "And what I was going to ask was: Is it true that your mother committed suicide?"

For a moment, Gail was unable to reply, trying to decide what signal had conveyed this truth to him. Finally, she asked him.

"None," he said soberly. "That was only a poorly placed joke. I simply recalled that there was an actress named Cressie Blake who married a very rich man named Gunnerson and subsequently killed herself." Gently: "She still appears on the Late Show now and then. Have you seen her?"

"No. I never watch my mother's old movies—I can't bear to. She seems like such a total stranger."

"That's too bad. If you watched them, you might see how I made my 'deduction.' "

"Yes, I know she resembles me."

"In any other way besides appearance?"

She met Vanner's eyes, feeling the necessity of holding a steady gaze. He broke it first, tugging at his beard. "Uh, were there any other relatives?"

"Only my Uncle Swann, my father's brother. And my cousin Piers, his son."

"Did you go to live with them?"

"No. My uncle traveled a great deal. Europe, mostly. But he arranged for my care—or at least, the Bank did."

"The Bank?"

"There's some money in the family. The Bank managed it for me—they still do. My mother arranged it

that way." With some bitterness, she added: "I suppose it's wrong to say I was an orphan. I had trust
officers for parents."

Vanner left his desk for the first time. His own
"body language" spoke of squash and tennis. He went
to the leather coat hanging on a hook and began fish-
ing for something in the pockets. When he spoke again,
his voice was free of bantering. "No, Miss Gunnerson,"
he said. "I doubt that a bank is much of a substitute
for a mother. You can't run to a bank when you skin
your knee, or feel lonely, or hurt, or bewildered . . ."
He faced her, the captured cigarette package in his
hand. "Or *scared,*" he said.

Gail waited.

"You were a frightened child, weren't you?"

"Yes."

"And the trouble is—you went and got yourself all
growed up. And you stayed frightened."

He came back to the desk, opening the pack.
"That's the unfair thing about becoming an adult.
You're supposed to put your childhood fears behind
you. Unfortunately, it isn't always that easy. That's
why people like me have diplomas and grow beards."

Something was scratching at the door, and Vanner
looked toward it and smiled. "Excuse me," he said.

He opened the door, and a furry bomb exploded in
the room, quickly employed the guidance system in
its nose to find the most interesting target, and ended
up licking Gail's chin. She laughed and fondled it and
asked. "What's his name?"

"*Her* name is Cassandra. Come on, Cass, leave the
lady alone."

"I don't mind, I love dogs. What is it? I don't know
the breed."

"Neither does Cass. Come on, Hairy, time for your
appointment!"

Cass bounded onto the doctor's leather couch, rolled over and stretched on her back. Gail laughed again; she was unfailingly tickled by anything mock-human that animals could do. Vanner went to shoo the animal off the couch, but the mutt was reluctant.

"Come on, Cassie, that's enough. Get off now."

"She likes it there," Gail said.

"Sure, she does. It's very comfortable. But it's reserved for people." He looked at Gail meaningfully. "For my patients," he said.

Gail absorbed the look in his eyes, and then stood up. "I get your message, Doctor."

As soon as she approached the couch, the dog bounded off. She said: "I have the feeling I've been tricked."

"Yes, you have," Vanner said easily. "But at least we're over that hurdle. Aren't we?"

When she emerged from under the apartment house canopy, she looked up and down at the almost deserted street and wondered why Park Avenue attracted so few pedestrians. Then she thought: It's the stores, or the lack of them; no window shopping. She kept her mind firmly on the examination of New Yorkers' walking habits and other minor topics; she knew she was preventing herself from examining the fifty minutes she had just spent in Dr. Joel Vanner's office; especially the last thirty of them when she had been forced, for the first time in years, to mention the Mead Clinic by name.

It may have been the thought of childhood that suddenly produced a craving for something sweet. She turned in the direction of Lexington Avenue and kept her eyes peeled for a coffee shop sign. Her concentration once again prevented her from becoming aware of being pursued. But she was.

She decided on a cafeteria, where she could spend more time making a selection from the dessert tray and *see* what she was getting. Ever since she was a child, Gail had to *see* a dish before her frail appetite could . . . Again, she forced herself to reject all thought of childhood; it was enough for one day.

At the counter, she selected a seven-layer chocolate cake, picked up a cup of coffee, and chose a small table against a wall. There weren't many other customers, so when the thin young man wandered among the empty tables, balancing a tray and looking lost, she immediately surmised that he was going to choose a table near hers. She was wrong. He chose *her* table.

"Mind?" He smiled, putting down his tray. It contained a cup of black coffee and a crescent-shaped sweet roll.

She looked him up and down—Gucci shoes first.

"Go away," she said.

"Public cafeteria," he said. "Supposed to share, you know."

"There are two hundred empty tables. Go away or I'll call the manager."

"I just don't feel like eating alone. I hate to eat alone. That's why I go to cafeterias, just to be with people."

"On second thought," Gail said, dropping the words like ice pellets, "I might even call the police. I'll tell them that you've been following me all day."

"All right, call the police," he said. "I'm sick of running away, anyhow. I'd rather shoot it out with them right now."

He sat down, and Gail reacted as if on springs, rising and grabbing her own tray.

"Please, Miss Gunnerson!" he said. "Don't go away. Sit down or I'll kill myself."

He picked up the crescent roll and aimed it at his head.

"How do you know my name?"

"I know lots of things about you. Your first name is Gail. You're taking drawing lessons at the Art League. You live in the biggest house on Schuyler Avenue. And you don't sleep well at night. Maybe it's all that chocolate cake you eat."

"And who are you? How do you know all these things?"

Gravely: "Miss Gunnerson, have you ever heard of the FBI?"

"Of course."

"So have I. Great outfit, isn't it? Wouldn't mind working for them someday."

"If that's supposed to be a joke—"

"It's not one of my best, no."

"You've been following me. Is that your idea of a joke, too?"

"No," he said. "It's my idea of a *job*. My name's Steve Tyner, by the way." He waited, expectantly. " 'Glad to know you, Mr. Tyner,' " he said. " 'Likewise, Miss Gunnerson.' "

"Who would hire you to follow me?"

"The word is to *protect* you. It's all very benevolent, believe me."

And now, of course, she knew. Words like "protect" evoked images of only one source.

"The Bank," she said flatly. "You work for the Fiduciary."

"Correction. I'm a self-employed investigator. The Bank hired my services, not me."

"What's the difference?"

"Mr. Tedesco at the Bank thought it would be a good idea to find out what's bothering you."

"Who said anything is? Except you."

He took a breath. "Four times in the last month, you called the police."

"I only called them once. Mrs. Bellinger called them those other times. My housekeeper."

"At your request."

"I heard . . . noises in the house. I thought it might have been a prowler, a burglar, something like that."

"And what did the police think?"

"There was nothing missing, no trace of anyone, no signs of a break-in. They said I must have been mistaken. It just didn't worry them."

"Well, it worried Mr. Tedesco. You know the Bank is interested in everything that happens to you."

Annoyed, she said: "The Fiduciary Bank, Mr. Tyner, is like a fat old mother hen. Every marble column in the place trembles when I sneeze."

"They're doing their job, too. Looking out for you— and your money. You're a rich little girl."

"Yes, and if they don't stop bothering me, I'm going to *buy* the Fiduciary and turn it into a laundromat."

"Were you satisfied by the police investigations? Did they manage to convince you that it was all your imagination?"

"Oh, I see," Gail said, thinning her lips. "You're a private investigator, and you don't mind soliciting clients in public places. Is that what it's all about, Mr. Tyner?"

"You've already got me on your side; how do I convince you of that? Look, even if the cops didn't find any jimmied doors or footprints in the pantry, the possibility exists that what you heard and felt in that house was real. That someone has his eye on the place, that he's making exploratory moves—a rehearsal for opening night. Of your wall safe and so forth."

"I don't have a wall safe. Except for the silver and some personal jewelry, I don't keep valuables in the house."

"There's *one* very valuable object in that house."

"What's that?"

"You," Steve Tyner said. "It's not just grand larceny we have to watch out for, Miss Gunnerson, there are other crimes. Like kidnaping and extortion. If these . . . problems you've been having are leading up to anything of that nature—you need close watching."

She stood up again, pushing her tray against the wall to make an emphatic sound. "Sorry, Mr. Tyner. I'm not hiring today. And you can tell Mr. Tedesco I've stopped hearing noises in the house, that I'm sure I won't hear them again."

"I'll have to tell him more than that."

"All right. Then tell him that I hate his phony paternalism, and his financial mumbo jumbo, and his dirty, rotten, spying detective *finks!* No, never mind. I'll tell him that myself, this afternoon. That if I ever catch sight of you again, Mr. Tyner, my account will be withdrawn from the Fiduciary on December second. If the date doesn't mean anything to you—ask Mr. Tedesco. It means a great deal to him!"

"Hey," Steve said weakly. "You're putting me out of work; you know that?"

"You know what I suggest?"

"What?"

She picked up the crescent-shaped pastry and handed it to him.

"Shoot yourself!"

She left the cafeteria so hurriedly, she almost forgot to pay her tab. Steve watched her disappear through the revolving doors, and leaned back with a sigh. He looked at the pastry in his hand, and put it to his temple.

"Bang," he said.

"It's her birthday," Tedesco told him.

"So what?"

"It's not an ordinary birthday, not according to the terms of the trust fund her father set up for her. She takes over full control of it then. If she really *wanted* to kiss the Fiduciary goodbye, she could. Now do you understand?"

Steve picked up a paper knife from the banker's desk and cleaned his fingernails with it. If Saul Tedesco hadn't been married to Steve's aunt, and if he didn't like him so much, and if he was as marble-hearted as Gail Gunnerson thought, he might have frowned at him. As it was, he actually smiled.

"Don't think I'm worried," he said. "Miss Gunnerson and the Bank have been associated for too many years for her to do anything so rash. It would be like cutting an umbilical cord. She may rant and rave about us, but she needs us, too."

Steve said: "I saw that cop again, you know."

"Baldridge?"

"Yes. I thought it wouldn't hurt to talk to him once more. He wasn't too pleased to see me."

"What did he say?"

Steve shrugged. "Same as he did before, only not so politely. He said every call was checked out throughly. The fact that the Gunnerson girl had cried wolf once or twice before didn't make them any less responsive; what else could he say? Oh—he had one more piece of evidence against her."

"What was that?"

"It seems she made another complaint two months ago, and not from her house. She was in a hotel upstate; there was a tennis tournament she went to see or to play in, he wasn't sure which. She called the local police in the middle of the night and said that someone had tried to break into her room. They checked it out, but there was nothing."

Tedesco sighed. "They know her history. Did I tell you that?"

"Baldridge hinted about it. Who told him, you?"

His uncle looked injured. "Why do you keep hinting that I'm conspiring against Gail Gunnerson? I'm not. I'm genuinely interested in her welfare. We all are."

"Uh-huh. You, and Mr. Comfort, and Mr. Sankey, and Mr. Rorimer, and all the little auditors . . ."

"Just do your job, Steve, that's all we ask."

"It's not as easy as it sounds. If she catches one more sight of me—I mean, she one tough cookie."

"You can make her crumble. Turn on the charm."

"You know what she called me? She called me a fink."

"That bother you?"

"Why should it? I *am* a fink."

"What did you tell her?" Tedesco said. "About yourself?"

"I told her that I was hired to protect her."

"In a way, you are."

"That's a kick. I'm spying on her, that's all it amounts to."

"It shouldn't bother your conscience, Steve. The girl will be taken care of, no matter what the courts decide . . ." He leaned across the desk and took the letter opener out of his hand, his voice soft with reassurance. "Look at it this way," he said. "The Gunnerson estate is a lot more than numbers in a bankbook. It's property, real estate, factories—the jobs of several thousand people—"

"And a nice fat account for the Fiduciary."

"Sure, it's that, too. But remember that we keep the machinery running, Steve. If this girl isn't well-balanced, responsible—she could do a lot of damage to that machinery. Grind it to a halt, perhaps. We can't let that happen."

Steve, his thin, nervous hands deprived of the letter knife, stilled them by shoving them into his coat pockets.

"You haven't even asked me what I thought of her."

"In what way?"

"My impressions of her, as a person."

Tedesco twisted his mouth into half a smile. "I warned you that she was pretty."

"I talked to her, Saul. She sounded straightforward to me. There wasn't anything hysterical about her. No big staring eyes, nothing at all like what you've implied to me."

"Implied? What have I ever *implied* to you?"

"You know damned well what you implied. All that talk about her being in a mental institution when she was a kid—a six-year-old kid, for the love of Pete!"

"She was almost twelve before they let her out of Mead," Tedesco said dreamily. "Half her life at the time. Then there was her mother. The medical records are pretty blurry about her, but she was obviously melancholic; that's why she hanged herself. Things like that run in families, Steve, didn't you know that? Hell, don't let those beautiful brown eyes fool you, just because they don't *stare*. No matter what you'd like to think—Gail Gunnerson is a mental case."

Three

Night thoughts:

The unfinished still life in the glassed-in porch her mother had called the Conservatory. Mixing apples and oranges on her pallet. Mrs. Bellinger, the maternal critic, cooing over the painting. *That fruit looks good enough to eat, honey.* But not good enough to frame, Gail told her pillow wearily. Punched it, turned it over to the cool side. —

Vanner. What time was her appointment tomorrow? Three or four? She had forgotten. What was the significance of that? Resistance, of course. Should she mention it? Gail moved her bare legs across the smooth sheets, suddenly aware of their sensuous texture. The words *bedside manner* came into her head, and she wondered if the association was erotic. Vanner was an attractive man. His beard had repelled her at first, but now she wondered how it would feel to the touch. She decided she wouldn't reveal these thoughts on the analyst's couch. She wasn't ready for transference—not yet.

Steve Tyner.

She blacked out his image by pressing her eyes against the pillow, but now the percale felt warm again. Or was it her flushed skin? Indignation, or something else? She began to resent her own train of thought. *Stop the train,* Gail murmured.

Sleep eluded her. Should she take a Seconal? Phenobarb? Nembutal? Choice of one, please. Nice Mr.
Todd, the too-cooperative pharmacist. Oblivion helpfully provided by kindly old gentlemen. And Dr. Yost.
What had he suggested for her nerves? A change of
surroundings. Escape from the familiar. Retreat from
the fearful. The doctors at Mead thought differently.
There was no escape, they said. This was her home,
and Gail should make it homelike again, a place of
peace and welcome, not fear.

Fear.

She opened her eyes, and let them wander about the
bedroom, to the window, to the hulking armoire, to
the door. She felt nothing. The darkness of her room,
mitigated by the glow of the night light, was comforting, not fear-inspiring. She had trouble making
Vanner understand why she didn't fear the dark. What
she feared was . . .

What?

She looked at the clock's glowing face. Two-fifteen.
She remembered the book she had started at midnight
and abandoned at one without penetrating its plot.
She groped for it now, but stopped when she heard the
bump.

It was an unmistakable thudding sound, as if
something round and soft and solid had landed
squarely on the Gunnerson house. A meteor, burned
out and softened into a cold ball of clay, falling on
her roof.

She heard it again, and knew that the sound was in
the attic.

Gail had heard noises there before, and each time
had allowed herself to be persuaded by a different ex-
planation. The dormer window was faulty. Old beams
and floorboards groaned and creaked. Gravity was
a mischief-maker, and piled-up boxes fell of their own

accord. More than one exterminator had warned of
termites. And then there were the rats, or the cats, or
the bats, the nonpaying boarders of so many attics in
so many houses of the Gunnersons' size and ven-
erability.

But each time the *thump* about her head made her
sit upright in bed and cry for the housekeeper. Mrs.
Bellinger once responded by calling the police (her
first encounter with the sour-lemon face of Lieutenant
Baldridge). Once by daring to visit the attic herself,
and giving Gail personal assurances that no demons
were at large. The third time, by simply holding the
quaking Gail in her arms and blaming it on a dream.

When she had told Dr. Vanner about the mysterious
phenomena, he had heard her out with solemn interest,
and asked if it had ever occurred to her to confront
them herself.

"I never knew there was anything to confront,"
she said. "I mean, I realize they must be nothing at
all . . ."

"You've realized it only secondhand," Vanner said.
"That's why you've never accepted the explanations."

"But I have!"

"Then why are you so afraid each time you hear
these noises? Why is each time a special event in your
life? Isn't it because you've never had the courage to
be your own observer?"

She thought about that now, sitting up in her bed
at two-fifteen in the morning, waiting for a repetition
of the thing that went bump in the night.

She heard it for the third time.

She was frightened, but she know what she had to
do. Instead of calling out for Mrs. Bellinger, she got
out of bed and put her robe and slippers.

She went out into the hallway. One end of it was still
guarded by the grandfather clock. The other side was

undefended. There was only a short flight of stairs that led to the attic door.

Dr. Vanner would be proud of me, she thought.

She climbed the stairs.

I don't even feel afraid, she said to herself, almost in exultation.

She opened the small louvered door. The attic entrance wasn't tall enough to admit a full-grown adult without his stooping, and she let that fact deter her for a moment.

The darkness inside seemed different from her bedroom darkness. But she knew that a light bulb dangled from the center, and the switch could be reached without venturing a foot inside.

She put her hand inside the door and found the switch, clicking it on with some effort. Disuse had stiffened it. There was no immediate flood of light; the bulb was of low wattage and the attic interior glowed yellow.

She bent her head and walked in.

Underneath the dusty circle of light, her mother was hanging from a low rafter, the electrical cord black around her white throat, and she was wearing the dress Gail remembered best, a floor-length sheath of shimmering blue satin.

Mrs. Bellinger was struggling with her. Why was Mrs. Bellinger fighting her, trying to pin her arms? Baffled, aware of protesting cries from her own throat, the angry pounding of blood in her ears, she screamed at her to stop, telling her that she had no right, no right at all! For a moment, she thought the housekeeper was going to slap her across the face, and remembered that was the remedy for hysteria, and realized that Mrs. Bellinger wasn't her opponent, only

her therapist. *It's me, it's me,* Gail thought wildly.
I've gone mad!

She resigned her struggles at the thought, and felt
the housekeeper's grip lighten on her arms. There was
a painful pressure against her lower back, and now
Gail saw that she was at the landing of the attic stairway, arching her body against the steps.

Then she remembered the cause of her hysterical
attack, and tried to tell her.

"I know, honey, I know," Mrs. Bellinger said
soothingly. "Only it wasn't, it wasn't. Come see for
yourself, darling, see how it was only your imagination."

She was trying to pull Gail back to the attic, and
Gail resisted with the pitiful whine of a child. (Piers
Swann trying to make her view the remains of her
mother. *No, Piers, no, I won't go in there!*)

"It wasn't what you thought, honey," Mrs. Bellinger said coaxingly. "Please come and see what it
was, please."

She was being led by the hand, back to the attic
door, back to the yellow-glowing room, back to the
apparition hanging from the low rafter . . .

She whimpered, but she looked.

Her mother's blue sheath dress hung from the beam,
supported by the black wire of a metal hanger.

"That's all it was, Gail," Mrs. Bellinger said. "You
saw her dress, not your poor mother. Anybody could
could have made that mistake, honey. Anybody."

Four

"No," she told Dr. Vanner the next day (her appointment turned out to be at four). "Mrs. Bellinger was wrong. Not anybody could have seen what I saw."

"I think I know what you mean," he said. "Hallucinations are very individual things. Made up of old buried images, apperceptions, private fears."

"Maybe that's what I mean," Gail whispered, her knuckles white on the sides of the couch.

"Talk about it," Vanner encouraged.

"That word—hallucination. Is that such a common experience? When people have hallucinations, doesn't that mean there's something wrong with them?"

"Everybody is allowed to *see* things once in a while. Some people go out of their way to see them. All the kids who drop acid, use skag, peyote, sunflower seeds —what do you think *they're* seeing by altering the normal function of their brain cells?"

"I've taken two puffs of a marijuana cigarette," Gail said. "That's all the experimenting I've done."

"All right. Let's just say that your eyes played a trick on you. And isn't it apparent that the reason they played this particular prank was because it was a scene you witnessed once before?"

"No." Gail shook her head. "I never saw my mother's body. Not when she hanged herself, not even afterwards. It was Mrs. Bellinger who discovered her in the attic." The line between her eyes deepened. "Come to think of it, I never knew *where* it happened. If I had known it was the attic, I never would have gone there last night."

"When did the recollection come back to you?"

"It didn't. Mrs. Bellinger finally told me. My mother hanged herself there with—with an electrical cord. When I was a child, nobody told me the details. They spared me as much as they could."

"Or you spared yourself," Vanner suggested gently. "You know that the mind has a way of forgetting things that it finds too unpleasant to remember."

"Yes," Gail said. "I know that only too well." She turned her head to look at him; Vanner's chair was always positioned just behind her head. "It is awfully warm in here, or is it just me?"

"It's you and me both," he smiled. "My air conditioner is in for a retread—that's why I have the window wide open. I was hoping you wouldn't notice."

"Is my hour almost up?"

"I still owe you ten minutes. Tell you what," he said cheerfully. "Would feel cheated and deprived if I suggested we finish this session outdoors?"

"Outdoors? Where?"

"The park. I promised Cassandra a long walk when the weather improved. We could stop at the zoo and have some tea or something. I don't have any more patients today."

"I thought analysts didn't socialize with their patients."

"That's what we tell them all. Except the pretty girls."

Cassandra, the approximate sheepdog, had a fit of almost uncontrollable excitement when they caught

sight of the first green rise. Vanner broke the city ordi-
nance by letting her slip her collar and go bounding after the other illegally unleashed canines. The sight of
her rompy, bouncy happiness made Gail feel better.

"It's lovely here," she said. "You ought to treat all
your patients in the park during the summer."

"Why not? I could have them lie down on the
benches."

They passed a snoring park bum, stretched out full-
length.

"Is that one of your patients?"

"One of my failures, poor chap."

Gail laughed.

But she was serious, even morose, when they were
finally served at the zoo cafeteria, Cassandra content-
edly asleep and dreaming of trees underneath the out-
door table.

"You know why I asked you that question, don't
you? About hallucinations?"

"Because you just had one, obviously."

"No. Because I've had *more* than one."

"You never told me about any prior visions."

She hesitated. "They don't all have to be visual, do
they? I mean, I've heard things in the house, noises
that probably never existed."

"What are you trying to say?"

"I'm saying that people who are normal, people who
are *sane*, don't have hallucinations."

"Are you referring to your mother?"

"You know I am."

Vanner sighed. "Gail, sanity and insanity are the
two most inexact words in Webster's. Next to 'love,'
that is."

"There was nothing inexact about my mother's illness."

Sternly: "From what you've told me, your mother

had an attack of acute melancholia following your father's death. That's the most common cause of depression, you know, the loss of a loved one. She needed help to restore her health, and she didn't get it in time. But you are."

"Yes," she said, and glanced at her watch. "I'm getting helped overtime. I didn't realize how late it was."

"Does it matter?"

"I have an art class at six. I'm going to be late."

"Will that be significant?"

"No," Gail said. "It won't be anything new."

But there was something new about her art class that evening.

"Extra added attraction," Helen Malmquist told her, nodding her head toward the opposite side of the room.

Gail looked. Steve Tyner was sketching at an easel. His concentration was obviously feigned. The moment she looked in his direction, he smiled and twiddled his fingers at her.

"Hey, that was fast," Helen said.

"Not really," Gail frowned. "That's the creep I've been telling you about, the one who's been following me."

"And you were complaining?"

Steve was removing his drawing pad from the easel and coming toward them, flapping the cover sheet to hide his artistic effort. He pretended not to look at Gail, but stopped at the easel of the woman beside her, squinting at her drawing with what he assumed to be a critical eye. "You know what's wrong, madam?"

The woman, surprised, asked : "What?"

"Your perspective. You have a natural left-handed perspective. You should always draw on *that* side of the room."

"You really think so?"

"Rembrandt had a left-hand perspective, too. Give it a try."

Even after he had possession of the easel, Gail refused to look at him. But the strain was too great. Refrigerating her voice to the best of her ability, she said: "Does the Fiduciary Bank know that they're paying for drawing lessons?"

"I've been painting for years."

"Pictures or ceilings?"

"Mind if I see your drawing?" Helen said, giving him a wide-mouthed smile. "It's all right. I'm with her."

"I didn't catch the name."

"Helen Malmquist. What's yours?"

"Steve Tyner," he said. "As a matter of fact, I don't like people to look at my work when it's still in progress. I'm rather sensitive to criticism."

"Maybe you should have taken private lessons."

"Maybe you're right." He looked tentatively toward Gail. "Can you recommend anyone?"

Helen looked amused at Gail's fixed attention on the nude model. She said: "What were you thinking of paying?"

"Oh, cocktails. Dinner. Maybe a hansom ride around the park. Think your friend would be interested?"

"Why don't you ask her?"

"Why not ask Mr. Liebling?" Gail said.

"I'm sure he's a great teacher. I don't think I'd care for him in a hansom."

"Sorry. I don't give lessons. I'm only a student myself."

"How about dinner anyway? Tonight?"

"Sorry."

"Lunch tomorrow?"

"No, thank you."

"Brunch? High tea? Coffee break? Midnight snack?"

Helen said: "Gail, Larry and I are going to the beach tomorrow. Why not make it a foursome?"

"Will you?" Steve said. "If I promise to leave the Fiduciary Bank at home?"

She continued to say no until he finally revealed the drawing he was working on. It was a stick figure with breasts. The moment she laughed, she knew they were going to the beach.

But the foursome didn't materialize. Gail was packing her suit and suntan lotion at ten the next morning when Helen called, her voice deepened by depression. She announced that "Larry," whoever he was, had suddenly found something better to do. Gail urged her to come along anyway, but Helen said: "No, thanks. Two's company, three's a French movie."

"Helen, what's the matter? Did you and your boyfriend have a quarrel?"

"No, it's nothing. It's just me."

"You're not on the flip side today, that's for sure."

"Yes, this is the other side of the record. Helen's Blues."

Gail considered calling Steve Tyner at the number she found in the phone directory, and canceling the outing. She didn't consider it long. She knew that she wanted this date, and not because of Helen's company.

Steve picked her up an hour later. On the slow, heavily trafficked drive to the shore, she told him about Helen's call.

"Does your friend get that way often? Depressed?"

"I haven't known her long enough to find out."

"And how about you? Do you get depressed sometimes?"

"That's between me and my analyst." She bit her tongue.

Steve, aware of her chagrin, said: "Nothing wrong with having an analyst. Still pretty fashionable, I understand."

"I'm sure you know all about him," Gail said flatly. "You and the Fiduciary."

"Sorry," Steve said. "I promised not to discuss anything you didn't want me to discuss."

"It's perfectly all right," she said, turning the refrigerator dial up a notch. "I don't mind answering your question. I *don't* get very depressed, not in the daytime, anyway."

"But at night?"

"Who doesn't, sometimes?"

"I'll bet you wouldn't if you weren't alone."

"I'm not alone. I have a housekeeper, Mrs. Bellinger."

"Great. And I'll bet you have a teddy bear, too."

"No. But I do have a Pooh Bear."

"Ye gods, another stuffed-animal nut. What makes women want to cuddle those silly toys, anyway? It's such a waste."

They were both hungry by the time they reached the beach. Mrs. Bellinger had packed the picnic lunch, consisting of fruit and ham sandwiches. Steve gallantly called it a luau.

"Where's the mustard?" he said, rummaging in the basket. "I can't find the mustard."

"Some investigator you are."

"Don't rattle me—it's my first job."

"What did you do before? I mean, before doing this dirty work for clients like Fiduciary."

"I used to work for a foreign news bureau. Pickering, do you know it?" She shook her head. "Before that I was a ship's reporter. I guess I like any kind of work that takes me places."

"So you're the roving type," Gail said.

"Never found anything to make me stay put." He found the mustard jar, and busied himself with it. "Or anyone," he added.

Half an hour later he went to the water's edge, and brought her back a cupped handful of the stuff. When he flung it at her, she cried: "Stop that! You'll get my bathing suit wet!"

They swam until the sky grayed over and then tackled a shore dinner at a restaurant too noisy for conversation. There wasn't much talk on the way home, either, but the silence was a friendly sharing of their tired, contented mood.

When they reached the driveway of the Gunnerson house it was only a few minutes after nine. Steve asked if he could come in. When she hesitated, he promptly spoiled things by saying: "I'd just like to look around the place. See if there's some way a prowler might be getting in and out."

"If *that's* why you wanted to come in," she said icily, "you can forget it."

"That was only reason A," he said hastily. "Reason B is, I intend to seduce you. Is that better?"

"Two wrong answers in a row, Mr. Tyner. Good night."

But when she entered the front hallway, there was a handwritten note propped up against the lamp on the hall table. She recognized Mrs. Bellinger's painstaking handwriting. The note read: *Gail—have gone to my sister's. Back before eleven, I hope. Love, Emma.*

The prospect of two hours of nighttime solitude made her react quickly. She opened the door again, and heard the crunch of Steve's tires as he turned to leave the driveway. The moment she reappeared, he squeaked to a halt.

"You can come in," she told him. "But only to look for prowlers."

Somehow, it took him a long time to reintroduce the topic. Despite the warm weather, Steve wanted to build a fire in the fireplace, blaming it on an atavistic, not romantic, impulse. In order to keep the room temperature reasonable, they had to turn the air conditioner on full blast. He also switched off lights and found a radio disc jockey who preferred pianists with a light, dusting touch on the keyboard. Gail accused him of creating a corny setting, and he admitted it. The only thing she refused to do was sit on the floor in front of the fireplace and play kissy-face. He suggested the couch instead. She countered by offering to show him her etchings. Drawings, actually. He said yes, without much enthusiasm.

"I started drawing when I was eight," she told him, spreading the cream-colored sheets on the coffee table. "It was supposed to be good therapy. I'm still not sure if I have any talent.

"Well, I don't know much about art," he said, slipping his arm around her waist. "But I know what I like."

That was when she suggested the house tour.

She was almost alarmed by the change that came over Steve Tyner as he began his inspection. There was no more flippancy in his manner. He explored the doors, windows, and locks of the Gunnerson house with a thoroughness that, if anything, exceeded that of the police examination. He asked her many of the same questions that Lieutenant Baldridge had asked her and seemed to know some of the answers before she voiced them. He took notes on the type and manufacture of each lock. He compiled a check list of entrances and required her to remember which were kept sealed and at what times of the day and night.

He explored the cellar, in her company, and the attic —alone. Then he asked to see the bedroom. She looked at him.

"Still Reason A." He smiled.

Ascending the stairs, he asked her casually if all the noises she heard emanated from the attic.

"No," she said.

"What else have you heard?"

"Just—sounds. You know how hard it is to tell where sounds are coming from. Sometimes I imagined they were in the hall, or on the stairs, or in a closet. Once I thought I heard my door opening, but that wasn't possible, of course."

"Why not?"

"I keep the bedroom door locked."

"With a key?"

She showed him the mechanism. "It latches from the inside. A key can open it from the outside, but only Mrs. Bellinger has one."

"Maybe it was Mrs. Bellinger you heard."

"No, poor thing. She has terrible foot problems, even if she makes a great show of being in perfect health. The last time the poor woman hobbled upstairs was—well, it was about three weeks ago, when I had a bad dream."

"Was that so unusual?"

"In this case, it was. We have an intercom between the bedroom and the kitchen, and the speakers were turned on by mistake. She heard me carrying on here and came upstairs."

"Would you mind telling me what you dreamed?"

"Now don't tell me the Fiduciary Bank wants to analyze my *dreams?*"

"No." Steve smiled. "We'll leave that to your Dr. Vanner."

"I see you've wasted no time finding out about *him*.

Did you break into his office for my files, like they did to Daniel Ellsberg?" She didn't say it lightly. Steve looked about for a distraction, and spotted the Pooh Bear. It was sitting up in a chair, its brown fur worn nearly bald from almost twenty years of embraces.

"So that's my rival, huh?"

"I won't hear a word against him. He's slept with me ever since I was a baby."

"Well, if he ever thinks of retiring . . ."

"I'll let you know when the job is vacant. Then you can fill out the usual application."

"What application?"

"At the marriage bureau," Gail said. When Steve winced, she added dryly: "Don't worry. If there's one thing I could never do is marry a private eye. And if that's what you are, Mr. Tyner, why don't you get on with it?"

But her bedroom yielded nothing out of the ordinary; or if it did, Steve didn't comment. He asked to see the bedroom next door, and asked who had occupied it last.

"My mother," Gail said.

"Did she spend a lot of time in it?"

"After her breakdown, yes."

"She wasn't ever hospitalized, was she?"

"No, she was treated at home. That was one of the advantages of having money, I suppose. Eventually, I think the family realized that a sanitarium was the only place that could really help her. But she was terrified at the thought of being . . . put away. She said she'd never let it happen."

"And she didn't," Steve said quietly.

"No. She didn't."

He started to leave the room, but Gail lagged behind.

"I know exactly how she felt, Steve."

"What's that?"

"I know how my mother felt. No matter how bad I get, I won't let them put a net over me. I'm sorry if that sounds melodramatic, but it's how I feel."

"Cut that out," Steve said. "Who's talking about *you*, anyway?"

"Right now, I'd say the Fiduciary Bank is. Talking a blue streak. Why don't you admit that they'd love to have me in a strait jacket?"

"You know that isn't true."

"They'd be tickled silly. They'd be able to play all the little fiscal games they wanted to with my money. Mr. Tedesco would be elected president of the Bank, and you'd probably get a bonus for proving that there's nothing wrong with this house that a padded room wouldn't cure!"

Steve marched toward her, grasped both arms, and did a flawless, cavemanlike, movie-star motion that pulled her up against his chest, and kissed her, not quite as flawlessly, bumping her nose slightly. In all other respects, the move was satisfactory. After her initial surprise, she returned the kiss, her arms circling him in the proper fashion. He was so grateful for her response that he kissed her for a third time. He would have kicked the bedroom door shut if his eyes hadn't fallen upon the Pooh Bear's disapproving face.

Tedesco was hanging a hunting print in his office when Steve entered it the next morning.

"That look straight to you?"

"A little lower on the left. Is that why you asked me here?"

"No," Tedesco said cheerfully. "It's a new assignment, Steve, and I think you're going to like it. A missing heir, a man named Applegard. Gets a hundred grand bequest from his grandpappy if we can find him."

"*New* assignment? What happened to the old one?"

"The Gunnerson case? Yes, that was a fine piece of work you did, that's what made me decide you were the one for this job, too."

"You talk like it's all over."

"Let's just say that *your* part is over and done with. I'm not saying we're going to institute any proceedings against her, but we've got more than enough ammunition when and if we make any moves. Now about this man, Applegard . . ."

"Wait a minute. Maybe my reports gave you the wrong impressions—"

Pleasantly: "Nobody asked you for impressions, Steve. Only the facts."

"The *facts* you have are purely circumstantial. It's only recently that I've gotten to know the girl personally."

"Yes," Tedesco sighed, "and to be honest with you, Steve, I think that wasn't your best ploy. You began to lose your objectivity, and that's a bad thing for an investigator."

"Are you sure the *Bank* is objective?"

Tedesco frowned and abandoned the picture-hanging. "I don't think I like the sound of that remark Steve."

"I still say it's crooked."

"What?"

"The picture. And what I meant was, you do have something to gain if Gail Gunnerson winds up mentally incompetent. Why don't you admit that?"

"Because it's not the truth. All we would gain is added responsibility, and very little additional income."

"But you're aware that Miss Gunnerson hates the

Fiduciary. That the odds are very good that she might change banks when she reaches the age of twenty-five and becomes custodian of her own fortune. But of course, if she was weaving baskets in some pleasant little drool factory . . ."

"Steve, if I didn't know you better, I'd say that was an ugly accusation."

He tried to keep his voice steady when he replied: "That girl isn't crazy, Uncle Saul."

Tedesco looked at him gravely, reacting to the use of the family name.

"All right, Steven. Nice, pretty girls like that aren't crazy. That would be very hard for someone to believe, especially if they've started to like that nice, pretty girl just a little bit too much. You think I don't understand that? I do. What I don't understand is why you can't appreciate the evidence that came out of your own research. Can you give me *any* other answer for all the things that have happened to that girl?"

Steve said: "All right. If you have to have another answer, I've got one for you."

"I'm listening." Tedesco sighed, and tilted the picture.

"I think someone's after her," Steve said.

Five

"I didn't know paranoia was catching," Saul Tedesco said, plumping himself back in the swivel chair.

"Is that the big medical decision? Is that the name your experts are going to give Gail Gunnerson's disease?"

"You know something?" the banker grunted. "When you fix your jaw like that, Steven, you look just like your father."

"Thanks."

"I didn't mean it as a compliment." Tedesco popped a candy mint into his mouth and sucked on it aggressively. "And what I meant was, it's obvious even to a layman that when a person thinks that goblins are haunting her, rapping on the furniture, sneaking around her attic, slipping poison gas under her door—"

"You never got that out of *my* reports."

"Let me remind you of something, young man. I called you in on this matter *after* we had received sufficient information to make us suspect that our Miss Gunnerson might be approaching the age of twenty-five with less than a full deck." He lifted his hand like a traffic cop when Steve started to speak. "Let me finish. When Theodore Gunnerson created his testamentary trust, he had no idea he was going to be creating it for an orphaned girl, and one with very special, uh, mental problems."

"At age six."

"The child is father to the man," Tedesco said gravely. "Or mother to the woman. Whatever happened to this poor girl in her childhood, whatever it was that put her into that mental home, it never just disappeared, Steve. Those roots went deep. When the Bank took over as her guardian, we were always aware that the problem might rise again."

"But you waited until *now* to take action. Just a short time before she takes control of her own estate."

"No," Tedesco said. "Gail Gunnerson waited until now, until about three months ago, when she started showing these paranoid symptoms."

"And now *I'm* showing them, right?"

"What would you call that statement you just made? About somebody being *after* the girl?"

"It's possible, isn't it? She's a very rich young lady. She's single. She lives all alone, practically. She's a natural target for the sharks, and the waters are full of them."

"What kind of sharks? Burglars, prowlers, second-story men? At our own advisement, the Gunnerson house contains little of value except the furnishings. No costly antiques, no precious jewelry, no large amounts of cash or negotiable securities."

"Great. Do all the second-story men know that?"

"Or maybe you're talking about fortune-hunters. Men who might want to marry the girl for her money."

"She's got more to offer than that."

"Well, well," Tedesco grinned.

"All right," Steve said flatly, "what about men? What's the status of her love life? I'm sure you know."

"Yes, we've always kept a careful eye on her romantic interests. Marriage would have altered our status, too. You may be interested in knowing that Miss Gunnerson isn't very active in that department. She's dated a few men, but she never kept a boyfriend more than a few months. I suspect she did the turning-off, probably when they drew a little too close. Let that be a warning to you."

"Look, I just met this girl. Stop implying things that aren't there." Tedesco seemed unimpressed by his denial. Steve said: "What I'd really like to know is—who gets her estate if something happens to her?"

"You, if you play your cards right."

"I'm serious."

Tedesco swallowed the remains of his candy mint. "Her next of kin does, of course. Her uncle, a man named Gilbert Swann."

"What do you know aboout him?"

"As much as necessary."

"Is he a wealthy man? Does he have the same kind of money Gail Gunnerson has?"

"Not to my knowledge."

"So he'd have plenty to gain, wouldn't he? If she was locked away in some sanitarium?"

"Nephew," Tedesco said soberly, "that's the second serious accusation you've made in the last fifteen minutes. If you think this girl's peculiar behavior is the result of some deliberate attempt to drive her crazy or such *Gaslight* nonsense, you're letting your imagination run away with you. Nobody would have anything to gain by such a preposterous action, not the Fiduciary Bank, not me, certainly not Gilbert Swann. The terms of the Gunnerson Trust prevent anyone but the trustees from taking care of her money—personal control by some greedy individual is just out of the question."

"Tell me about Swann anyway. Tell me where he lives, or how I can track him down."

Tedesco looked at his watch. "I have an appointment," he said. "I'll walk you out, Steve."

"I won't do anything rash. I promise not to involve the Bank. Any inquiries I make will be strictly on my own. I won't even send the Fiduciary a bill."

Tedesco clipped a ballpoint pen to his pocket, and rose. Steve followed him through the long corridors of the Bank, all the way to the exit. "Uncle Saul," he said earnestly. "I'm asking you this as a personal favor. At least make it possible for me to talk to this man. Just to satisfy my own curiosity."

Tedesco sighed. "I can satisfy your curiosity right now. If you think her uncle is involved in any way with these delusions and hallucinations, you're wrong. Gilbert Swann and his son have lived in Europe for the past *twenty-one years.*If you want to talk to somebody, Steven, talk to the girl's psychiarist."

Dr. Vanner gave Steve Tyner a measuring look. It was so penetrating that he felt the psychiatrist had just assessed his height, weight, average yearly income, and practically all his hang-ups. But he waited patiently until Vanner answered his question.

"Do *I* believe in haunted houses? No," he said. "But I *do* believe in haunted people."

"Is that what you'd call Gail Gunnerson?"

"I wasn't talking about Miss Gunnerson. And as I said, Mr. Tyner, I'm not about to, either."

"Look, I realize there's some ethical thing involved about revealing client confidences. But I thought you might be willing to make an exception in this case."

"Is that a request from the Fiduciary Bank? Or is it a private matter?"

"As I said, the Personal Trust Department of the

Bank hired me to keep an eye on Miss Gunnerson . . ." He frowned. "Look, I'll be honest with you,
this isn't strictly true. They hired me to report on
her behavior, to help them decide whether she was
mentally competent."

Dryly: "Are you qualified to judge?"

"All I did was report her actions. The interpretation
of those actions would be made by people like yourself, if necessary." He clasped his hands. "Personally,
I don't think it *is* necessary."

"So you *have* made a judgment."

"I'm convinced she isn't unbalanced. I think she's
high-strung, overemotional, sensitive. But I don't think
she's hearing spirit voices and seeing ghosts in her attic."

"She told you about that?"

"Yes."

"And of course, you promptly told the Bank."

Steve squirmed. "I had to tell them."

"Didn't you know they might use that information
against her? In any kind of sanity proceedings?"

"It was my job!"

"Does Miss Gunnerson know the exact nature of
this 'job?'" Steve's face answered for him. "I thought
not," Vanner said.

"Naturally, I couldn't tell her. That would have
been the end of any possible relationship."

"Or in the language of spy stories," Vanner said,
"you would have blown your cover." He dropped his
gaze to Steve's interlocked fingers. Steve parted them
guiltily, feeling naked and exposed in front of the analyst's eyes, beard, and diplomas.

"I'm telling you this in confidence, of course."

"Naturally," Vanner said dryly. "I realize that people in your . . . profession claim the doctrine of privi-
ledged information, just as they do in mine. But you

have nothing to worry about, Mr. Tyner. I won't remove your disguise. Not for your sake—for hers."

"How do you mean?"

"Gail talks about you, of course." Steve didn't miss the switch to her first name. "From her description of you, she's come to believe that you're a sort of guardian angel, even though you're on the payroll of the Fiduciary Bank. And right now, Gail Gunnerson is going through a critical period in her life. Any breach of faith by people she cares about could be . . . Well"—Vanner shrugged—"I can't believe you're insensitive enough not to realize how hurtful this realization would be."

"That's exactly why I'm talking to you. Because I don't want to see her hurt."

"That's easy to accomplish, from your standpoint."

"How?"

"Remove the possibility of disappointing her."

"You mean, get out of her life."

"Don't you realize that she's bound to learn the true nature of your interest in her, sooner or later? What do you suppose it will do to Gail, when she finds out you're a fraud?"

Steve got out of the chair, feeling an urge for a cigarette he hadn't experienced since Quit-day two years ago. Vanner watched him with all the Sphinx-like patience of the analyst, offering no secrets, only demanding them. Steve began feeling a healthy dislike of the man, and grudgingly admitted that the emphasis was on "healthy." He turned and said: "I know what's on your mind. You think I feel guilty about what I've done to Gail. Okay, that's the truth of it. But I haven't got the time or money for the full course of treatment, so do it for me in one paragraph, okay?"

"What would you like me to say?"

"Tell me whether this girl is mental or misunderstood. She's got to be one or the other, you know that as well as I do. Tell me that's just a cute little neurotic, and not a candidate for those rubber-sheet bathtubs, and I'll do everything I can to convince the Bank to lay off. By the way, he's my uncle."

"Who is?"

"Saul Tedesco, the trust officer who manages Gail's estate for the Personal Trust Department. He gave me the assignment as a favor when I quit my last job. I'm sure he doesn't want to hurt Gail, either; he's got a heart like a marshmallow. Toasted."

"Sorry," Vanner said crisply, "I wouldn't give you a conclusive paragraph about Gail Gunnerson, even if I thought it would call off those financial dogs that are snapping at her heels. She's been my patient for less than a month."

"But you must have some idea about her condition."

"I have ideas. I simply don't have all the facts."

Now Vanner was looking at him without the same stony impassivity, his eyes frankly speculating. "Actually," he said, "there might be some way you could be helpful."

"Me?" Steve said. "How? Try me. I'll do anything."

"Gail Gunnerson has the kind of problem that requires a 'breakthrough,' if you get my meaning. Perhaps a series of them. She's suffering from what we call 'circumscribed amnesia.' That is, there are blind spots in her memory that exist for very significant reasons."

"She mentioned that to me."

"She did?" Vanner leaned forward with quickened interest.

"She just said there were things about her childhood she can't remember. I hardly thought that was 'significant,' though. The only thing I remember before the age of six was spilling some hot cocoa in my father's lap, and hearing him scream: 'Jenny, he's ruined the best part of me!' "

"I'm not interested in your childhood. Only Gail's."

"Well, for one thing, she has no recollection about where and how her mother committed suicide. That the first time she learned the gory details was the night she thought she saw her mother in the attic."

"Not necessarily true, of course. That could have been one of the buried memories. In fact, I have to conclude that it was, considering that the hallucination was so specific."

Steve frowned. "You used the word 'hallucination.' "

"And *she* used the word *electrical cord* when she described what she saw. Wouldn't the natural assumption have been that her mother hanged herself with a rope?"

"Okay, so what if she did bury the memory? Isn't it better that she did?"

"Yes," Vanner said. "There are healthy burials of fact, and then there are unhealthy ones."

"Like what?"

Vanner picked up a pencil and tapped it on the desk. "The door," he said.

"What door? Of her bedroom?"

"Hasn't she told you about it? The fear she has concerning that door?"

"I know she keeps it locked, but that's all I know."

"Hasn't she told you about the night her mother died? The night she experienced something so terrible that it resulted in her forcible commitment to a mental institution?"

Steve hesitated. "I know she was sick as a child. I know it was connected with her mother's suicide, but that's hardly any surprise, is it? Her father had died not long ago. Her mother starts going crazy, and then takes her life. How well-balanced are you supposed to be at six years of age?"

Vanner placed the pencil on his desk and twirled it. When it stopped, the finely sharpened point was directed at Steve. "What has she said to you about the *door?*" he asked.

"Nothing."

"Didn't you know that Gail believes her door opened that night? And that some *thing* came through it, some *thing* that was so horrible to view that she drew a curtain over the memory that hasn't been lifted to this day?"

"No," Steve said. "She hasn't mentioned anything about it to me. Is that what she told you?"

"It's something I've learned through the inference of her own statements. And, I admit, by information I obtained through her past medical records. As you know, the file is very thick on Miss Gunnerson."

"Well, what of it? So she had a bad dream, and it scared the hell out of her."

"You know what trauma means, don't you?"

"Sure I know what it means. But I also know what nineteen *years* means in a lifetime. And that's how long ago this dream occurred."

"The doctors at the Mead Clinic never learned the details of that dream. So they were never able to analyze its meaning. Gail Gunnerson's unconscious mind built an incredibly stout defense to protect that memory from exposure. And frankly, I believe she's never going to be emotionally sound until that defense is breached."

"You mean you *want* her to remember this 'thing?' "

"Yes," Vanner said gravely. "I think it's crucial for her to remember what frightened her so much. The 'thing' has to be isolated, defined, and faced—not as a six-year-old, but as a woman of twenty-five, who can recognize the fear as insubstantial."

"And then she'll be cured?"

"Bad word."

"What if she remembers the *thing* and it still scares her? Maybe it'll drive her off the spool completely."

"When I said that you might be able to help, Mr. Tyner, what I meant was that Gail might lower her defenses for someone like you. She might reveal the truth, even without knowing it."

"I don't see how."

"This blind spot of hers—think of it as an animal, a wild creature that's taken refuge in her mind, cunning and savage and not easily trapped. It recognizes the enemy it has in *me*, realizing that it's my job to trap it. But in your presence, it might not be as wary. Do you see?"

"Look"—Steve frowned—"I'm having enough trouble learning to be an investigator, to say nothing of being a psychiatrist."

"The facts are fairly simple. The dream occurred on the night Cressie Gunnerson was removed from her deathbed for burial. Gail was in a terrified state; she refused even to take a last look at her dead mother, a fact which troubles her still. When she went to bed, the body had been taken away. In the middle of the night, she had this dream. All we know about it is that she saw the bedroom door open, and something unbelievably terrifying entered her room."

Steve was shaking his head. "I'm sorry," he said. "I know you're the expert, Dr. Vanner. But I can't understand why all this is such a mystery. Given the circumstances of that night, doesn't it seem obvious to you what the 'thing' was?"

"Does it to you?"

"Of course," Steve said. "My guess is that she saw

her mother come through that door. Her dead mother."

Vanner leaned so far back in his chair that the springs creaked. "Yes," he said softly. "That was his guess, too."

"Whose?"

"Her uncle's," Vanner said. "A man named Gilbert Swann, who handled the final rites for the family before returning to his home in London. The chief psychiatrist at the Mead Clinic wrote to him, and he expressed the same opinion in his letter of reply. It seemed as simple and clear-cut to him then as it does to you now."

"And what do you think?"

"Frankly," Vanner said, "I just don't know." Steve glanced at him, and respected the look of honest doubt, even of bewilderment, in the troubled gray eyes above the well-trimmed beard.

Cecilia Louise had put on a few extra pounds since Steve had seen her last, not to her disadvantage; he guessed that her last assignment had been in some good-food town.

"Paris," she said. "Isn't that super? I ate masses of food, darling; I was absolutely piggish." Her enthusiasm, as usual, broadened the English accent she had brought to America and the Pickering News Service a dozen years ago. Not all the enthusiasm was for her report, judging from the way she blinked her Wedgewood-blue eyes at Steve.

"I really meant to call you," Steve said. "But you know how it is when you leave a job under a cloud—"

"Cloud? That's a lot of four-letter word, and you know it. Pickering was devastated when you resigned, love; he wasn't in the least bit upset about that jeep business. Not that I ever heard the full story."

"Sissy, whatever you heard was true." Steve smiled. "I stole the jeep. It was the only thing I could do in the circumstances. Even if those Haitian cops wouldn't actually *say* so, I was a prisoner in that restaurant."

"It all sounds so thrilling." Cecilia sighed. "I've always been do *disappointed* about this foreign correspondent business. I thought we were all supposed to go around having terrific *adventures,* and you seem to be the only one who ever did."

"Wrong. Most of the time I did what the rest of us did, attended a lot of dull briefings, interviewed anybody I could, filed my cables, and tried to enjoy myself. The only reason I got so 'adventuresome' with that jeep was because I couldn't stand the thought of being under armed guard in that greasy spoon. The food was inedible. Fate worse than death."

"Oh, dear"—Cecilia sighed—"there we are back to food again. Can't we change the subject? How about sex?"

"How's Perc MacDougal?" Steve asked quickly. "Still in Sierra Leone?"

"No," Cecilia said. "He quit. As a matter of fact, the job is open, darling; Pickering would absolutely *love* having you back at work. Why don't you call him tomorrow?"

"No," Steve said.

"They're really desperate to find a replacement for him. All I'd have to do is *mention* that you're interested in coming back to work, and Pickering would do a half-gainer."

"No," Steve repeated. "The only person I'm going to call at the office tomorrow is you."

"Me?" she shrieked with delight. "Darling, you've finally realized it at last. You're mad about me."

"I'm going to call you for information, love. You're

going to use the vast resources of the Bureau to find
out something for me."

"Find out what?"

"About a man who lives in your old home town. A
man named Gilbert Swann."

He knew Gail was aware of his nervous mood when
he picked her up at seven the following night. His calls
to Cecilia, three of them that afternoon, had yielded
nothing. She claimed to be having problems unearth-
ing the information he requested; he half-suspected
that she was going to string out this business all the
way to another cocktail or dinner date. At the conclusion of his final call, she had suggested that he try her
at home that night; something might still come over
the wire at closing time.

At the dinner table, looking at the face whose
beauty seemed newly discovered each time he saw it,
he barely heard Gail's comment about the change in
her life, until she accused him of not caring.

"Not caring about what?" he said blankly.

"My decision," she said. "I know it isn't earthshak-
ing, but I thought you'd be interested."

"Of course I am."

"No, you're not. You haven't listened to one word
I've said all evening. I admit that most of my words
have been dull, but the last batch at least contained
some—what do you call it? Hard news."

"I'm sorry," Steve said. "Try me again."

"I've quit the Art League," she said. "I've decided
that I'm not only wasting my time there, but poor Mr.
Liebling's. I don't have a serious talent, Steve, and I
don't enjoy drawing enough to make it a hobby. Of
course, Helen is upset about it; she thinks it's a terrible
mistake. Do you?"

"No," Steve said. "I don't think it's a mistake, if it's how you honestly feel."

"I think Helen is the only reason I've stayed in the class as long as I have. I began to feel responsible for her, I think—especially after that breakup she had with Larry."

"Who?" Steve said, wondering where the restaurant pay phone was located.

"I never met Larry, so I can't tell you the first thing about him. But evidently he was someone very important to poor Helen, and when they finally broke up for good, she was almost demolished. I'm very worried about her, Steve."

"Listen," he said, rising from the chair. "Would you please excuse me for five minutes?"

"Of course." But when she saw him reach into his change pocket, she said: "Don't tell me you have to pay in the men's room? In this fancy place?"

"No," he said. "I have to make a phone call."

"Business?"

"No," he said. "Actually, I'm calling a beautiful blond young lady to see what she has to say for herself." Gail was smiling when he left the table; nothing like the truth to get you off the hook, Steve thought.

Cecilia sounded mournful when she answered the phone.

"I know," he said. "You still haven't learned anything. Well, just keep after it love; it's important."

"Darling, I didn't say that. The truth is, I *have* found out something about your friend, but I thought you wouldn't be terribly happy to hear it."

"What do you mean?"

"Oh, dear," she said. "One *hates* to be the bearer of bad news. Don't they call us harbingers or something nasty like that?"

"Sissy, will you please tell me what you learned?"

"He's dead. Gilbert Swann is dead, darling. Was he a very good friend of yours?"

"No," Steve said, feeling that the phone booth was sinking into the wine cellar. "I never knew the man. How long ago, do you know?"

"Six months ago. He and his son Piers were killed in Zurich, Switzerland, in a landslide or something. Listen, darling, if I were you I wouldn't be alone at a time like this. Why don't I rush right over and stroke the fevered brow?"

Six

"I don't *know* why I'm crying," Gail said, dampening Steve's shirt pocket with her tears. "It's just an awful thing to hear about. Can't you understand that?"

"Sure," he said soothingly, stroking her hair and taking advantage of her emotional state by drawing her closer to him than she usually permitted. "I just don't understand why you didn't get any official notification of their deaths."

"I suppose nobody thought of notifying me. Uncle Swann and his son lived in Europe for such a long time, all their connections were there. I'm not sure anyone even knew that he had a niece in the States. How did *you* find out?"

"Just a routine inquiry," he said casually. "The Bank needed a question answered, about the date of a document, something like that. That's when they learned about the accident."

Her tears were downgraded to sniffles now. She rose from the sofa and went to find a tissue.

"I like that," Steve said.

"What?"

"The way you blow your nose. I'm very sensitive to things like that, the ways girls sneeze or cough or laugh. I was almost engaged to a girl once, but then she caught a cold and I heard her sneeze and cough. Argh. I knew I couldn't put up with that the rest of my life."

"You're trying to cheer me up," Gail said accusingly.

"Sorry. Tell me some more about your uncle. Why did he live in England, anyway? Or was it because he *was* English?"

"No," Gail said. "My father's family *did* come from England, originally, but that was several generations ago."

"Then Swann was your father's brother."

"Yes. I know very little about him, except that I gather he was something of a snob. Antiquarian, Anglophile, very correct, not very lovable. He loathed this country. I remember reading an old letter he wrote to my father, calling America one great big hamburger stand, surrounded by fat people in station wagons . . ."

"Mind if I speak ill of the dead? I don't think I would have liked your Uncle Swann."

"Neither did I," Gail said. "Even if I did meet him only once."

"The time your mother died."

"Yes. Although I suppose he was around when my father was killed in Korea. I just don't recall. But he returned here when my mother—when she died—and arranged the funeral and so forth. He brought his son with him, Piers. A bratty kid. I hated him, too."

"And yet," Steve said gently, "I've got a wet and salty shirt."

"I couldn't help crying about it. Do you realize that this means I have nobody now? Not a single living relative in the whole world?"

"Are you really sure? I'll bet if you ran a classified ad—'rich young lady seeking relatives'—you'd have a thousand third cousins popping up all over the country."

"No," Gail said. "There's nobody, Steve. Maybe that's the cause of all my neurotic problems. Maybe if people don't have any human attachments, they come loose, like untied balloons . . . I'll have to ask Dr. Vanner about that."

Now it was Steve's turn to leave the sofa. He went to the fireplace and looked at the fresh timber Mrs. Bellinger had placed in the grate. As if to discourage further summer fires, she had stuck folded paper fans between the logs.

"You think a lot of this analyst of yours, don't you?"

"As a matter of fact, I do."

"Would you be upset to know that I paid him a visit?"

Her silence made him turn. "Or maybe he's already mentioned it," Steve said.

"No, he hasn't." A light nip of frost. "Did you ask him not to tell me?"

"I guess I suggested it, yes."

"Well, he honored your request. Now would you honor one from me?"

"Sure."

"Tell me why you did such a thing. I mean tell me honestly. Did you go there on the Bank's behalf, or on mine?"

"Want the truth? I went for my own sake. I wanted to see what I could learn about you, about this problem you're having. And about my own problem."

"What problem is that?"

"I didn't want to bring the subject up in this context."

"It's up."

"There's something sad about a cold fireplace," he said. "Hey, what's the point of all the paper fans? Looks very mid-Victorian."

"Will you please answer me?"

"Actually, I guess they're a kind of kindling, is that it? If you fold paper, it burns longer."

"Steve!"

"All right!" he shouted back. "I've been wondering if I'm good or bad for you. And vice versa, I guess —although there's been very little vice in our relationship, come to think of it."

"Is that why you went to see Dr. Vanner? To complain about my cold fireplace?"

"I just wanted to check him out, that's all. You'll be pleased to know that he's an ethical type. Wouldn't discuss his patient with me. In fact, he was so protective of you, I couldn't help getting some nonprofessional vibes."

"What does that mean?"

"I think he likes you, and not for your case history. Didn't you say he's a bachelor?"

She watched him suspiciously. "I don't know whether to believe you or not. Something tells me you're just covering your tracks, like a good flatfoot should."

"Speaking of tracks," Steve said, "I'm getting hungry. Didn't you say you were willing to try that Szechuan restaurant? Why don't we do that?"

"No," Gail said flatly. "I don't think I'm interested

in anything that hot and spicy. And if you want to think that's a double entendre, Mr. Tyner, go right ahead."

"There's no reason to be sore at me."

"Isn't there?"

"Gail, so help me, I didn't see Vanner because the Fiduciary suggested it. Now let's go back to Square One and start this evening all over again."

"You never asked me if I had *other* plans for this evening," Gail said. "The truth is, I was thinking of visiting Helen. She's been very depressed, as I told you. She asked me to come over tonight, and I think I will."

"I thought you were depressed yourself. Because of your uncle."

"Birds of a feather," Gail said.

"Wrong maxim," Steve said. "What you mean is, misery loves company." He looked miserable himself as Gail went to the telephone.

Helen Malmquist's apartment building was on the West Side, a monotonous brick pile, depressing in its lack of character. Gail regretted her decision to make this call the moment the shirt-sleeved "doorman" greeted her with a lecherous smile, holding a paper bag molded around a wine bottle. But Helen had sounded so overwhelmingly grateful at the idea of the visit that Gail steeled herself for an evening of social work.

Surprisingly, Helen's mood was determinedly gay.

"What the hell," she said. "Larry was getting a bald spot. He's only twenty-eight and the stuff is going fast. He would have been a billiard ball in another three or four years."

"There's always a bright side." Gail smiled.

"Sure, that's right. Although come to think of it,

maybe *I'll* be bald in three or four years, if I keep going to that same colorist. Her name's Olga—I think she's a Russian agent, boring from within. Which probably describes me right now, doesn't it? Boring?"

"No," Gail said. "Of course not. Listen, Helen, I'm only sorry it took me this long to get around to seeing you again. Are you still going to the Art League?"

"Yes, I'm still going. But I don't enjoy it very much. I think the best part of the whole thing was having someone to talk to."

"That's funny," Gail said. "I told Steve the same thing."

"Then you're still seing the private eye."

"Yes."

"Does it look serious?"

"I don't know."

"*You* look pretty serious. In fact, you look the way I'm supposed to look. What's the matter?"

"Nothing," Gail said. "I heard some bad news today about some relatives of mine. They were killed in a skiing accident in Switzerland."

"Oh, wow, that's too bad. And I asked you over to make *me* feel better. You're not going to have to go abroad, are you, for the funeral or anything like that?"

"No. It seems to have happened months ago, but I just learned about it today. They're not people I knew at all, Helen—I didn't mean to introduce morbid topics."

"Why not?" Helen lit a cigarette and the pungent odor made Gail start; it also explained her friend's relaxed mood. "That's one of my favorite things, morbidity. You don't know how often I think about death. Or maybe I'm just willing to admit that I think about it. Maybe other people won't be truthful about their private thoughts. Want a drag?"

"No, thanks," Gail said, wrinkling her nose as the smoke trail brushed her face.

"It'll do you good. You've smoked before, haven't you?"

"Yes, once. I didn't care for it."

"Maybe you'll like it better the second time. This happens to be very fine grass. Go on."

Gail took the joint reluctantly, accepting the offer only as part of her social service.

"You can finish that," Helen said. "I have half a dozen more, all rolled and everything. Courtesy of the late lamented Larry Rosenbaum, henceforth known as Baldy Rosenbaum." She found another cigarette in the drawer of the coffee table and lit it up. "His last remains, going up in smoke." She giggled. "See what I mean? You can't get away from the subject; it always comes up, like sex."

"What subject?" Her first puff made Gail's head spin.

"Death, of course. Don't you think about it?"

"I suppose so."

"Be honest. Don't you think about it a lot? What it'll be like, not being alive any more?"

"I don't suppose we realize that we're not alive any more—when we're dead, I mean." This struck her as funny, and she laughed.

"I don't know, I just can't buy that," Helen said. "The idea of not *feeling* or *knowing*. That's just too much to accept, just an endless kind of nothingness. Everything comes to an end, right? I mean, if life ends, maybe death does, too."

"That's an interesting way of putting it," Gail said, feeling slightly sick to her stomach. But she kept on smoking, and realized that her two previous experimental puffs on a marijuana cigarette hadn't give her any notion of its brain-bending possibilities. Maybe it was because she hadn't eaten since breakfast, or because she was anxious to escape Helen's topic, or simply because she was disturbed by her conversation with Steve, and the fact that he wasn't with her now, and that they had half quarreled and would that mean they would only half make up? She giggled, or Helen did; she wasn't sure which.

"You know what I think?" Helen said, her right hand doubling in size as she lifted the cigarette to her lips. "I think death is a terrible misunderstood thing, I honestly do. The trouble with death is, it doesn't have a lobby." Her head was shrinking slightly now, but her eyes remained the same size, enormous brown orbs that never seemed to blink. Gail watched them with interest, waiting for the lashes to flutter, but they never did. "What I mean is," Helen said, "nobody ever speaks up for death—everybody's against it. What we need is a committee or something, a *movement*— maybe we should have bumper stickers and lapel pins, you know? "Death Power." How does that sound?"

"Awful," Gail said. "It sounds just terrible, Helen. Excuse me—the bathroom?"

"It's somewhere around here."

Gail rose unsteadily. She didn't have to search very long, however. Helen's apartment consisted of a narrow entryway that was diminished by a massive chest of drawers, topped by a gold-leafed Buddha. The room they sat in was a box designed for living, dining, and assuming that the bamboo shade concealed a wall kitchen, meal preparation. There was a door, too, and Gail assumed it led to the bedroom and the bath. She had some small trouble negotiating her way toward it, and wasn't helped by hearing Helen's warning: "That bedroom lamp is out, honey, careful."

But she found the bathroom, a hanging garden of

hosiery, and searched for the switch, found it, flicked it on, and light crashed into her, exploded around her, filled her eyes and ears and mouth with its brilliance, blinded her, but not before she saw her mother's face in the mirror, death's own reflection, and then: darkness to scream by.

"Oh, honey, honey," Helen crooned, rocking her in her arms. "Don't be upset, don't be. It was just the bulb, the stupid *bulb* blew out; that's all it was. You're okay, Gail, honestly . . ."

"Oh, God, I was so afraid," she said. "It was a bolt of lightning, like *ten* bolts all at once, and then I saw —something—"

"You couldn't see *anything*," Helen said. "Not after that. You were like a kitten who was just born when you came out of that bedroom. You should have *seen* your eyes, honey . . ."

"I feel so stupid." She looked guiltily at Helen, whose own eyes were unfocused, and she remembered the "good grass." Then she laughed, a quavery sound she didn't recognize as her own. What was it Steve had said, about girls with funny laughs, snores, and sneezes? No, he hadn't mentioned anything about snores. That would have to wait, Gail thought, wishing she could stem the laughter that was shaking her body. "No more for me," she told Helen. "I'm just not a pot smoker, Helen that's all there is to it. The Surgeon General has determined that pot smoking is dangerous to my health."

"Are you sure you're all right now, hon, are you really sure?"

"Yes," Gail said. "You know what my trouble is? I'm just hungry; I'm absolutely starved. I haven't had a thing to eat since breakfast."

"That's what always happens." Helen giggled.

"When you smoke grass, you get this horrible appetite. You can smoke yourself fat. That's the biggest danger if you ask me, Surgeon General. Listen, I don't have a thing to eat in the house . . ."

"No Szechuan?" Gail said. "No Szechuan at all?" She removed herself from Helen's arms and went to the phone. "It's all right, I have a friend. I *used* to have a friend."

Somehow, she managed to dial Steve's number.

"You know what?" he said. "You sound high."

"I'd *have* to be, to call you," Gail answered with dignity. Then she remembered her mother's face in the bathroom mirror, and her voice began to quiver again. "I have to see you," she said meekly. "I'm having an anxiety attack or something. I was going to call Dr. Vanner, but he doesn't know about the Szechuan restaurant . . ."

Steve said sternly: "Stay where you are and I'll pick you up. And no more booze, or whatever it is."

"How dare you talk to me like that," Gail said.

"I'm in love with you," Steve said. "That's how."

Seven

She wore a peach-colored cotton voile dress with a low neck, back and front. It was especially good against the dark brown of Vanner's leather sofa, and Gail looked down at the full skirt and matching sandals with the satisfied knowledge that she had to be making a good impression. Then she realized that the doctor would want to know what she was thinking, and quickly tried to take her thoughts elsewhere. A little too late, however.

"You were smiling," Vanner said.

"Was I?"

"Very definitely. And very prettily, too. As a matter of fact, you look especially pretty today. Summery and all that."

"It's summer, isn't it?"

"Yes. But you haven't really dressed for it, not in my office, anyway."

"It didn't seem appropriate in these clincial surroundings."

"And suddenly—it's appropriate?"

Gail blushed, and knew he would make psychological capital out of the fact. "I just felt like buying some new clothes," she said. "I told you about this hang-up of mine about clothes. Or non-hang-up, I suppose, considering how empty my closets are." Vanner was chuckling. "Well, the millennium is here," Gail said. "I made you laugh."

"Don't congratulate yourself. Patients who try to amuse their analysts usually do it to avoid facing serious topics."

"I wasn't trying to amuse you. I was just telling you how I felt. That it was time for me to take an interest in my appearance."

"I'm sure you realize that's healthy."

"You should be pleased with me, then."

"I am," Vanner said. "Very pleased. If a little distracted. But that isn't your problem, it's mine."

Her neck hurt with the strain of resisting the impulse to turn and look at him.

"It's all right," he said. "You can comment on that if you like. I once told you not to be surprised to discover that I'm human. Also male, unattached, heterosexual, and susceptible." He added a smile to his voice. "Fortunately, I can add one more adjective. Professional. At least I'm trying to be."

"You know something? I think I'm being complimented, but I'm not sure."

"You can take it on face value. I'm pleased with you, Gail, and not just because of the way you look."

"You mean because of my dreams."

"Yes. How long has it been since the last bummer?"

"More than a week now. In fact, I haven't dreamt at all for the last three nights—I've slept like a child. No," she said, smiling, "a little less like a child, actually."

"How do you mean?"

"It's silly. I mean that I haven't taken my Pooh Bear to bed." And added quickly: "Or anyone else for that matter."

This time, Vanner's laugh lasted longer. "Welcome to the Gail Gunnerson Comedy Hour."

"I'm sorry. I'm really not trying to hide anything. I know you want me to be truthful about my love life, but it's the subject I find most difficult to be explicit about."

"I think that's explicit enough. You're telling me that you haven't slept with Steve Tyner, at least not yet. Isn't that correct?"

"Well—since we're on the subject, no. I haven't. And he isn't forcing the issue, either."

"What do you make of that?"

"I think he understands how I feel. That I tend to overcomplicate my relationships, that I'm not ready for involvements that I can't handle."

"You associate sex with involvement?"

"Of course. Don't you?"

"Let's remember who's on the couch, okay?"

"Sorry," Gail said.

The office phone rang.

"I thought I'd turned that damned thing off," Vanner said.

He crossed in front of her toward the desk, his face fixed in a frown, and snatched the receiver from its cradle. "Hello?" His eyes rolled upward at the response. "Yes," he said, with controlled exasperation. "Of course I am. I just happened to leave the phone switched on by mistake, or else the service would have taken the call . . . I'll be through in about fifteen minutes, and then I promise to talk to you, all right?" Gail could hear a persistent, female-sounding buzz in the telephone diaphragm, and it began vibrating at higher frequency. "That's absolute nonsense, Helen. You're doing this just to get sympathy."

Gail sat up at the mention of the name.

"I'm not lying to you," the doctor said, in a tone of parental chastisement. "As a matter of fact, the patient is your friend Gail, and I'm not going to deprive her of the attention she's paying me for." Now Vanner looked worried as well as annoyed. "Helen, please listen to me. I can't possibly come over there now. After Gail leaves, I have another patient to see. Lie down and don't think about anything, just shut your eyes and try to relax . . . Yes, just as soon as I can. I promise."

He hung up, with a deeper frown than the one he had started with.

"Helen Malmquist?"

"Yes," the doctor said. "She wanted me to come and see her. Just drop everything and go over there."

"What's the matter?"

"She's depressed. I don't know if you've been in touch with Helen lately, but she's had a disappointment. With a young man."

"Yes, I know. Larry."

"It seems to have triggered a lot of her old self-doubts. Frankly, it's been something of a setback for both of us." Vanner flicked his beard with the one nervous gesture he permitted himself. Then he looked at Gail and said: "I don't suppose I should tell you this, but since you *are* her friend—there was a time when Helen Malmquist was—"

He paused, and she intercepted with: "I know what you're going to say. Helen told me about it herself—about her suicide attempt."

"I'm sure she'll never retrogress that far, but when someone even *hints* about taking his life, I'm usually inclined to take him seriously."

Gail gasped. "Is *that* what she just said?"

"Not in so many words. She was less than coherent, actually. She might well be on something, alcohol or grass or even downers. I just don't know."

"But that's frightening. Shouldn't you do something?"

"I don't think it warrants calling the police or anything like that." He looked at his watch. "And I *do* have a patient coming shortly, someone in almost as much trouble as Helen is. I'd hate not to be here when he arrives, although I suppose I could postpone the session."

"Would it help if *I* went over there? Just to make sure she's all right?"

"That's kind of you," he smiled wanly. "But you haven't had *your* money's worth, either."

"No, really, I'd be glad to do it."

"Well—all right. I'm sure your presence would be soothing to her. Make her some tea or coffee, keep her calm. Talk to her about movies, hairdos, anything trivial. I'll get over there just as soon as I can get rid of my next appointment."

"Maybe it's good therapy," Gail said lightly, "helping other people. Neurotics Anonymous."

"Maybe so," Dr. Joel Vanner said.

The elevator in Helen's building operated jerkily, and its plastic green sides were sweating. Gail thought: If I lived here, I'd be miserable, too. But of course people lived in worse places in this city; Gail had been spared the grinding down of poverty and would never really know it. She realized how infrequently she appreciated this blessing. And others, come to think of it. She glimpsed a watery reflection of her peach voile dress in the shiny elevator wall, and thought: I'm an attractive woman. I know I am. Pretty, damn it. And I don't have any ailments or illnesses or deformities. Why should I travel through life in the company of so many black clouds? Why? It was a strange place for a lightning flash of revelation, but it seemed to be happening to her, midway between the eleventh and twelfth floors of the apartment building on the corner of West End Avenue and Eighty-fourth Street.

She rang the bell of 12-G without summoning any response. She tried it several times, refusing to think the worst of things. Helen didn't know she was on her way over; Helen could have gone out, shopping for milk, eggs, bread, downers; Helen was asleep, narcotized by whatever she was using. Gail pushed the button a few more times, and then turned away. Halfway to the elevator, her rational explanations gave way to doubt, and she wondered if she should ask the wino doorman to let her into the apartment. The thought of the explanations she would have to give him changed her mind. Helen would have to live with the embarrassment for as long as she remained in the building. Then another thought. Why did she assume that Helen's door was locked? Of course, it should be

—the name of this city was New York. But Helen was blithely careless about such things, walking home alone from the Art League at all hours, swinging her purse invitingly, tempting a fate that had so far been obligingly kind.

She went back to the door of 12-G, and tried the knob.

The door was open.

Gail walked into the narrow entryway and saw the gold-leafed Buddha. Helen's household god was being used as a prop for a sheet of drawing paper. Even before she could make out the words, Gail knew that it was a notice meant for the eyes of the next person who came through the front door.

Her hand trembled when she picked it up.

A felt-pen scrawl. *Sorry, everyone,* it said.

Helen's handwriting, the bold stroke of her penmanship, bolder than her drawing line.

Sorry, everyone, the note said. *This is the only way for me. Nobody's fault but Helen.*

Gail put down the drawing paper and said: "Helen?"

She refused to admit that the word was wasted breath.

She walked into the living room—empty. She entered the bedroom. It was empty, too, but the door of the bathroom was open wide.

Gail went toward it, determined to see nothing but its sterile interior, white tiles and porcelain and chrome.

Please, she said to herself. *Please.*

But Helen was there.

She was draped over the tub, wearing a white cotton nightgown that had absorbed her blood like a gauze bandage, making streaks and blotches all the way to the hemline, dull-red in color. But the blood on the tiled floor, the blood still moving in a slow current toward the bathroom drain, that was bright, bright red. The mouth of the crimson river was her left wrist. The right had evidently been slashed as well, but had no more to give; that hand rested outside the tub. Not far from its curved fingers was a shiny rectangle of steel, its edge tinted. It was astonishing how much fine detail Gail was able to observe; she could almost read the name of the manufacturer on the single-edge blade. Where was the blurred vision that should accompany shock? Why couldn't she make this crimson-red reality disappear? Whatever happened to the precious gift of her childhood, the ability to bury the sight of terrible things? Why was she seeing this now, and screaming?

"Gail! *Gail!*"

Two firm hands on her upper arms. She realized there must have been a moment of amnesia after all because she didn't remember when Vanner arrived. But here he was, shaking the hysteria out of her body, the way Mrs. Bellinger had done. Here was the doctor, substantial and comforting, and she was grateful for the sight of him, and what was it Helen had said to her once—God bless every hair in his beard . . .

"She's dead," Gail sobbed, clutching at him, needing the wall of his body to support herself. "She killed herself, she really did it! We came too late . . . too late . . ."

"I never should have let you come here alone," he said, and she realized that his agony was more for her than for Helen. "I was wrong to do that, Gail. I came after you the minute I was able to put off my next patient."

"Could we have stopped her?" Gail said. "Was there anything we could have done?"

"Stop including yourself," Vanner said. "She was my responsibility, and one that I simply couldn't handle." He moved her away from him gently, turning her face so that she was spared any further view of the body. "But the least I can do is keep you out of it now. Go home, Gail. I'll take care of reporting this. There's no reason in the world why you should be involved."

"Yes," she whispered. "I couldn't bear that, I couldn't stand talking to the police. I just want to go home."

"And to bed," he said firmly. "You can consider that doctor's orders. Go to bed, take one of the pills I prescribed, and don't budge until you hear from me tomorrow morning. Is that understood?"

"Yes," Gail said, but still clung to the sleeves of his coat. He looked at her quizzically, and then leaned forward and covered her lips with his. It was more like a benediction than a kiss, but it had a calming effect on her. She left the apartment and headed for the elevator, hearing the distant voice of Vanner on the telephone, make the announcement to city authorities expert in handling horror as statistical reality.

She didn't cry again until she was home, and Mrs. Bellinger, bunions and all, insisted on seeing her into the bedroom and waiting until the sedation took effect. Mercifully, that was soon.

Eight

Dreams:

Bicycling on a dark country road, desperately trying to keep the wheels tracked along the luminescent white line, lurching black elms arching overhead, an endless tunnel of trees, narrowing into oblivion . . .

A man following her down a street in Nowhere, tattered tweed coat so long it dragged on the pavement, blank-idiot face at the nape of her neck, hoarse voice whispering obscenities in her ear . . .

A room with chalky-white walls and no furniture, a cracking, tearing sound as bits of plaster scaled from the ceiling and showered down on her; sobbing because her party dress was ruined, crying out for her mother, hearing her footsteps in the hallway, realizing there was no door, no way in, no way out, pounding on the walls, crying . . .

Gail opened her eyes.

No country road, no limbo street, no chalky-white room.

She was safe in her own bed. Wry thought: Why were people considered safe in bed? Sickbeds, deathbeds, no-bed-of-roses beds. Beds where nightmares were stabled. Tried to remember the dream details, and failed. Tried to analyze meaning, failed again. That would be Vanner's job, she told herself. To decode the symbols. Decipher the anxieties. Her eyes closed again. Drifting back to the rim of darkness.

She was almost there, in the realm of nonawareness, but something brought her back.

A sound.

She didn't move. She lay still, wishing ears could be shut as easily as eyes.

Again.

She turned slowly in the bed, twisting the sheet around her body (winding sheets, thoughts of death), inched herself upward against the headboard, concentrating on the bedroom ceiling.

But the sound wasn't in the attic.

It was at her door.

"Mrs. Bellinger?"

A light tapping.

"Is that you, Mrs. Bellinger?"

She left her bed, went to the door, unlatched it. She looked at the knob, expecting the housekeeper to turn it from the other side, but nothing happened. She decided she was wrong. She had been tricked by misdirection once more. Tricked by Sound, the party magician. All right, Gail thought. She would turn the knob herself, and give the magician his satisfaction.

She opened the bedroom door.

Helen Malmquist, in her bloody nightgown, was on the other side. At first she appeared to be no more than a standing corpse. But then her red-smeared sleeves were lifted slowly, and her dead-white hands were extending toward Gail, dangling limply from the deeply gashed wrists.

"Come with me," Helen said.

Nine

Mrs. Bellinger had never been so glad to hear a phone ring in her life. She forgot corns, bunions, and calluses in her sprint toward the instrument, and her athletic effort was rewarded by the sound of the correct voice on the other end.

"It's Dr. Vanner. My answering service said Miss Gunnerson called me."

"No," the housekeeper said, trying to catch her breath. "It wasn't Gail who called, Doctor, that was me. She's in a terrible state, and I thought you should be called instead of some regular type of doctor. Oh, you know what I mean," she said in contrite confusion. "She talks about you all the time, about how you're helping her over these bad dreams and such. Only this was the worst one, Doctor. This wasn't like any of the others . . ."

"All right, Mrs. Bellinger, just take it easy. This *is* Mrs. Bellinger, I assume?"

"Yes, sir, this is me, and what I was going to ask was if you could come over, or should I call someone else, like her medical doctor, Dr. Yost?"

"I really can't answer that until you tell me exactly what's wrong, Mrs. Bellinger. Could you possibly put Miss Gunnerson on, so I could talk to her?"

"No," she said, "I can't do that. I mean, she's

asleep, finally. I don't want to wake her up now. She was like a crazy woman when I went up there, Doctor, sobbing and shaking like I've never seen her before; if you could have been there—"

"Please, Mrs. Bellinger," Vanner said, exquisitely patient. "Tell me exactly what happened."

"But that's what I don't know. I mean exactly. I heard Gail scream—really *scream*—and she wasn't in her bed, even, she was at her bedroom door. She opened it and screamed like the Devil himself was in her room. I came upstairs as fast as I could, and there she was, laying there in the doorway, passed out cold."

"She fainted?" Now Vanner's response seemed more appropriate, and Mrs. Bellinger continued eagerly.

"Out *cold!*" she said, with dramatic emphasis. "And white as a sheet. And all sweaty and clammy, you know? I practically had to carry her back to bed, and she began talking so wild . . ."

"Was she delirious?"

"I wouldn't know what you call it. Nothing she said made any sense, but I guess that's how it is with dreams."

"Are you sure it was just a dream, Mrs. Bellinger? Couldn't it have been another hallucination?"

"I just don't know," the housekeeper said. "Gail said it must have been a dream, that's all I can tell you."

Vanner seemed surprised. "Gail told you that? Then she *did* become coherent?"

"Become what?"

"Mrs. Bellinger, this is very important. Was Gail able to talk to you after all this—was she able to make sense?"

"Yes. Yes, she was sensible enough, but if you

could have seen the way she looked, like death warmed over, and the way her whole body was shaking . . . I mean, it's summer, Doctor, and I had to dig out the electric blanket for her and turn it on medium high so she could warm herself up . . ."

"I see," Vanner said, in a worried voice. "The only thing is, Mrs. Bellinger, I doubt if it would do any good for me to come over, now that she's asleep. It's best that she pass the rest of the night undisturbed."

"I'm not sure she'll do that."

"Do you know if she took any of the medication I prescribed?"

"No, I don't."

"Well, in all likelihood she won't wake again until the morning, and then we can decide what to do."

"Something *has* to be done, Dr. Vanner—you know that, don't you?"

"Yes," Vanner said, just before he hung up. "Something must be done." But his last words were addressed to Helen Malmquist, who sat cross-legged, pouting, on the edge of the sofa, her stained negligee pulled up over her knees. Vanner's expression was one of faint disgust, as if he found the combination of the sexy pose and gory costume in excessive bad taste.

"Why don't you wash up and change?" he said. "I can't stand looking at you."

"Gee, thanks, that's always nice to hear," Helen said, reaching for a cigarette. "But don't forget who designed this little number, Herr Doktor."

"I mean you've got to get dressed anyway. We have to get you out of here, and the sooner the better."

"What's the hurry? Miss Millions isn't going to come calling, is she? This is one place she won't be in a hurry to visit again. Do you want a drink?"

"No," Vanner said, and watched her slide off the sofa, spilling half a dozen pillows to the floor in the process. She went to the long bamboo blind that concealed the wall kitchen, and rolled it up, revealing a sinkful of dirty dishes, some of which he could identify from the scraps as three days old.

"Well, what did the housekeeper say?" Helen asked. "From the way you looked, it wasn't what you wanted to hear."

"Everything is all right," Vanner said doggedly. "You know it's all right; you saw the effect on her yourself."

"Wrong. I didn't wait to see any effect. I told you. The second I saw her knees give way, I backed off and got out of there as fast as I could. I was scared stiff that she would make a grab for me, and then what?"

"She fainted," Vanner said. "Passed out cold."

"And now?"

"She's sleeping. The medication is still working in her, of course. Naturally, she'd go back to sleep."

"And that's all? She didn't flip out completely?"

"She was delirious when she came to—that's what the housekeeper told me. But she managed to calm her down and get her back to sleep."

"Great," Helen said, twisting her wide mouth. She poured two inches of bourbon into the bottom of a glass that could have used another rinsing. When she slid the ice cubes into it, she said: "It isn't working, is it? Your foolproof plan?"

"Of course it is," Vanner said. "It's just that you can't make up a timetable for something like this—it has to be flexible, creative."

"Creative!" Helen laughed. "Now there's a word."

"In this case it's the right word. It's like psychoanalysis in a way. I mean, what do you think analysis is really like? It's not a cut-and-dried process, a system that goes from A to Z and that's that."

"God help us," Helen said. "Herr Doktor is lecturing again. You know how sick I am of hearing you sound off on that subject?"

"Maybe you think I don't know what I'm talking about."

"Show me a real diploma," Helen said harshly, "and maybe then I'll let you lecture me." A sip of her drink and her mood changed. "I might even lie down on the couch for you," she said, her eyes coquettish over the rim of the glass.

"It's going to work," Vanner said stubbornly. "It's just a matter of time."

"You're kidding yourself. That's how I analyze *you*, Doctor. You like to kid yourself. Well, don't feel too bad about it—so do I. The way I look at it, kidding yourself is an occupational disease. Occupation meaning living."

"The housekeeper said she was hysterical," Vanner said, almost to himself. "Talking out of her head. Even if she didn't go off the deep end completely, she's obviously halfway there."

"But that's not far enough."

"No," he said, "not quite."

"And you were so sure of it," Helen said mockingly. "So damned cute and so damned sure. You had the whole thing *analyzed*."

"What I knew for *sure* was that she was afraid of death."

"Who isn't?"

"But it was worse for her; it was something that never left her mind. Don't you see? This thing that happened to her when she was a kid, when she was only six years old, it put a warp in her brain that's still there. It's *got* to be there."

"And if it isn't—no payoff, right?"

"It's there," Vanner said, tugging at his beard. He took the glass out of Helen's hand and sipped—made a face. "How can you drink that stuff?"

"It's American as apple pie, Herr Doktor. Sorry I don't have any schnapps. Would you like some wine?"

Vanner didn't answer. He made a circuit of the boxlike room, planting furrows in the thin nap of her carpet. "I thought I knew what Gail saw that night. I was sure the 'thing' at the door was her dead mother. That she dreamed her mother got out of her death-bed or her grave and came waltzing into the room . . ."

"But she never *told* you that."

"No. She didn't tell anyone, not me, not all those other doctors who took care of her . . ."

"Those *other* doctors. Boy, you're really getting schizoid about this, honey. You're believing your own lies now."

"You know what I mean. She spent years in that clinic; I told you about that. And she was never able to describe exactly what she saw. And when I introduced the topic—same problem. Complete, total blackout."

"What makes it so damned important?"

"It is," Vanner said, coming to a halt. "It's the trigger that snapped in her brain the first time. So why not again?"

"Why didn't you give her truth serum or something? Wouldn't that have worked?"

"They tried some drugs on her when she was a kid, but she reacted badly. When I hinted at it, she got her back up. Even if she agreed, I think her resistance would have been too great for any useful result."

"So Herr Doktor is up against the wall."

"Stop calling me that," Vanner said. "You're wearing that joke pretty thin."

"Maybe we're wearing this whole thing too thin. Maybe what you're trying to do is impossible."

"No," he said. "I still have faith in the plan. We've just had a few setbacks, that's all. Like this romantic attachment of hers—that hasn't helped. This all-American boyfriend of Gail's has shored her up, given her more self-confidence."

"And he's cute, too," Helen said.

"I can get rid of him, of course. I know just the formula. But I thought he might be useful—I thought he might be able to provide me with a clue of some kind."

"About the 'thing'?"

"Yes," Vanner said. "I told him how important I thought it was; I tried to recruit him to discover what's hidden in her mind." Wryly: "Strange sort of ally, but it might work."

"How long are you going to wait?"

"It can't be too long." Vanner frowned. "This situation can't continue. For one thing, it doesn't fit the parallel."

"What do you mean?"

"I mean the parallel between Gail's mother and herself. At the time her mother went crazy, there wasn't any man in her life. She lost her husband in Korea. There was nobody around to take his place, nobody for her to reinvest herself in."

"My," Helen said, "you do use fancy language, darling. You might even have convinced *me* that your diploma was real."

"It's the central fact. Gail has been worried about this parallel between herself and her mother ever since she was old enough to think about such things. There *is* such a thing as hereditary insanity."

"And do you really believe she's going the same way?"

"It's what *she* believes. If *she* sees the parallel, sees herself heading for that padded room, maybe she'll choose the same solution that her mother did."

"No," Helen said flatly. "That's the part I can't buy. That she'll do you the big favor of killing herself."

Vanner had stopped listening again. "Maybe I shouldn't wait to act on Tyner. Maybe I should put a spike in him right now, so there's no obstacle in the way of her doing . . . the right thing. It might even give her more reason for making the move. If she loses him. It would help the parallel."

"Are you sure that's your only reason?"

"What are you talking about?"

"Sometimes I wonder about you, Doctor. About what's really going on in that head of yours. I mean, for all I know, what you're actually planning to do is marry the girl for the money. That would be just as good, wouldn't it?"

"That's nonsense."

"Maybe you thought you could make her so dependent on you that she wouldn't be able to live without you."

Now Vanner thought she was worth some attention. He moved toward her, slipped his arms around her paint-smeared negligee, smiled down at her. "Forget it," he said. "Nothing like that ever entered my head. Gail Gunnerson is only good to me dead. We're still a team, Face."

"You haven't called me that since Europe." Helen pouted. "You haven't said the poem since Europe."

"Is this the face that launched a thousand ships?" Vanner said, "and burnt the topless towers of Ilium?" He slid the negligee upwards over the arch of her curved body, and buried his beard like a spade in her neck. "Sweet Helen," he murmured, "make me immortal wih a kiss." She moaned softly, dreamily, and

he brought her to the sofa with a gliding step and lowered her to the cushions. He didn't seem repelled now
by the gory red smears of paint on her wrists and
arms and negligee; the simulated bloodstains seemed
to excite him, and Helen was ignited by his fire.

"Oh, Herr Doktor," she whispered.

"Stop calling me that," he said. "You know my
name."

"Oh, Piers," she said.

She was in the shower half an hour later and heard
him enter the bathroom, heard him fumbling in the
medicine cabinet, and called out over the sound of the
drumming water to ask him what he was doing.

"Making sure there's nothing left behind," he said.
"Things that belong to me. No shaving cream or anything like that."

"What? I can't hear you."

"Never mind," Joel Vanner, born Piers Swann,
said, and continued his methodical cataloguing. He
was totally absorbed in the process, enjoying thoroughness for its own sake. He was fanatical about neatness
and order; the headmaster of his prep school in Kent
had called him "compulsive" in the stiff letter to his
father that resulted in still one more change of venue
in his education. In the breast pocket of his coat, there
was a small notebook bound in the thinnest of English
leathers; in an exquisitely fine hand, Vanner had a
coded list of every important detail of the scheme he
had dubbed Operation Golden Door, a name which
amused him only so long as it remained secret; not
even Helen Malmquist, his one and only confederate
and confidante, knew it existed. He had once thought
of calling it Operation Defrost, since it had been born
and nurtured in an abandoned alpine cabin made
inaccessible to civilization until the spring thaw. He

had spent the two coldest weeks of his life in that cabin, still not completely certain whether his father was alive or dead after the slide had abruptly ended their mountain adventure. But perhaps the cold had served a purpose. Wasn't it true that cold did something to the cerebrum? Shrinking it diamond-hard, perhaps, and enabling the mind to carve out crystal-clear thoughts and brilliant strategies? Weren't all the great movements of art and science and philosophy born in atmospheres of low temperature? Not that Vanner had worked out all the fine details in his two-week hibernation. At the time, he hadn't counted on the willing assistance of the penniless American art student he had met in Zurich, who was only too happy to cooperate in his Get-Rich-Quick plan, once she recovered from the initial shock of learning that Piers was (a) alive, and (b) bearded. He hadn't worked out all his delicious bits of theatrics, the strobe light exploding in the bathroom, the photograph of Gail's dead mother mounted on the mirror, the hanging mannikin in the attic, the bumping, clanking, creaking hauntings and humbuggery that were made possible by the simple expedient of employing the full set of Gunnerson house keys his father had left him as his only real legacy. The most risky moment of the operation took place when he returned anonymously to their London flat on Fulham Road, and found his father's creditors busily appraising Gilbert Swann's meager treasures. But all had gone smoothly after that, and he was still confident of a happy conclusion to Operation Golden Door; when he swung the medicine cabinet shut, he smiled at his own reflection in the mirror. Then he saw Helen's reflection as she stepped out of the shower, wet and steaming, her glistening skin accenting the plumpness of her body, and he realized that in a few years she would probably, and cheer-fully, go to fat.

"Would you hand me that other towel?"

He did, and watched her dry herself carelessly, her eyes pensive and her wide mouth downturned. "What's the matter?" he said. "Why do you look that way?"

"I can't help it. I just can't stop thinking about it, Piers. I can't convince myself that it's working, that it'll ever work. She's too young, she's too damned pretty, she's too *rich*. People have to be in a lot worse shape than that before they'll consider suicide."

"Wait and see," he said.

"And she's in love," Helen said gloomily. "I know she is, I can tell by the way she looks whenever she mentions that guy's name. Since when do girls in love knock themselves off?"

"When they lose their lovers, maybe? And what do you think will happen when she learns the truth about Steve Tyner? Learns that he was hired by the Fiduciary Bank to prove her crazy?"

"No," Helen said, shaking her head, spraying him with water particles. "She'll get upset about it, maybe, but she'll forgive him, Piers. Women are like that. We suffer you bastards, don't you know that? Even the worst of you. And if you want to see a good example, look in the mirror."

Vanner looked. This time, no smile was reflected. "Stop worrying about it," he said coldly. "I told you that I have it worked out, all of it. There's no possi-bility of failure."

"Look, you may be her 'analyst,' but I'm her 'friend,' and I know her as well as you do. She's got too much going for her, Piers. She's not going to believe she's nuts, just because you want her to!"

"And what about other people?"

"What?"

"You may be looking at this with too narrow a focus. What will *other* people think when they hear reports of her hehavior? Such as seeing her dead 'friend' Helen walking into her room?"

"What does it really matter what they think? It won't do you any good if they *commit* Gail, for Pete's sake. That won't get you the inheritance."

"I'm not talking about committal. I'm talking about their *acceptance* of her death, about their willingness to believe in the motives for her suicide."

"But if there *isn't* any suicide—"

"There'll be a *death*, and that's just as good. A death completely justified by her frame of mind."

It took Helen a full five seconds to understand what he had just said, and when she did, she drew the bath towel about her with a sudden chilling of her flesh. "What does that mean exactly? A death?"

"Just what it sounds like. Gail has to die, or the whole thing has been a waste of time. And if she won't be cooperative enough to do it herself, she'll simply have to be assisted."

"My God, I can almost believe you're talking about murder." She threw the bath towel on the floor and reached for the long terry robe hanging from the hook. She didn't look at him when she put it on as if she was afraid to see what his expression would reveal. But when he continued to remain silent, she turned and saw exactly what she feared to see. "Pier's, for God's sake, *that* isn't what you had in mind all along, is it?"

"Just as a last resort," he said easily.

"You wouldn't! I can't believe you'd do anything like that! You know I wouldn't have any part in something like that! It's bad enough *this* way, but murder? Boy, have you got the wrong vampire!"

She belted the robe more tightly, and left the bathroom.

Piers opened the medicine cabinet. He went through
it again, as methodical as ever.

Ten

"It's just no use." Cecilia Louise sighed, looking like
a doe at a salt lick as she touched the rim of her Mar-
garita glass with her tongue. "It's just like that American writer said, about not being able to go home again.
What was his name? Thomas something."

"Wolfe," Steve supplied.

"Which doesn't begin to describe you, love. I've done
everything except print an engraved invitation on my
mattress, and it hasn't done the slightest bit of good.
It's terribly depressing, really." But her appetite unaf-
fected, she assailed her enchiladas. Steve made another
furtive attempt to see the face of his watch, an enterprise hampered by the restaurant's dim candlelight.
This time, she caught him at it. "You want to call *her*
again, don't you?"

"Who?"

"Darling, I know exactly where you disappear to
every time you leave this table. You must have made
three calls to that woman since we came into this place.
Please don't forget that you're dining with a trained
observer."

Steve smiled and said: "I told you there was a girl in my life these days, Sissy."

"But you didn't tell me she was an obsession."

"The truth is, I'm a little worried about her. I called her just before I left my apartment—that would have been about seven o'clock. Her housekeeper said she was in bed, asleep."

"So what's wrong with a siesta? Ask the people who run this restaurant, darling; those short naps are wonderful."

"It's not so short. The last time I called she was *still* asleep. I think that's carrying a siesta a little too far. And besides," he frowned, "I didn't like the sound of the housekeeper's voice. I can't help thinking that something's wrong over there."

"Your girl isn't sick, is she?"

"No," Steve said hesitantly, "not exactly."

Cecilia covered his hand and gave him a motherly look. "Listen, love, I never thought there was much hope of kindling the old flame between us—don't think I was that silly. Now tell me all about her."

Steve, who couldn't recall much of a conflagration, gave her an affectionate finger-squeeze nevertheless. "Sissy, you know that information you got for me, about Gilbert Swann?"

"Of course I remember, darling; that's why you're buying me this lovely dinner, out of gratitude."

"Mr. Swann happens to be her uncle. That's why I wanted to know what became of him."

"Oh, dear. And is that why she's all broken up, sleeping at nine o'clock in the evening? Because she's upset about her uncle getting himself killed?"

"She didn't really know the man, but he *was* her only living relative, him and his son, and now that they're both gone, she's fresh out of kinfolk . . . By the way, did you get any further details on the accident?"

"No, but I could keep after it, if you like." She patted his hand. "Now run along and make the call. Tell her you're on the way to see her, courtesy of Mama Louise. I'll just sit here and drown my sorrow in Sangria."

But in the phone booth, Steve's only reward was Mrs. Bellinger's voice again. "No, I'm afraid she isn't," she answered. "Like I said, I think the best thing is for you to call her tomorrow morning."

"You think she'll sleep through the night?"

"Well, she might," the housekeeper said. "In fact, I hope she does. The truth is, Gail isn't feeling very well. She had a bit of a scare tonight and she needs some rest."

"What kind of scare?"

"I don't think I should talk about it."

Steve said: "Will you talk about it if I come over there? Mrs. Bellinger, I really think I have a right to know."

"Please! Let the poor girl sleep. She was half out of her mind tonight—I had to call the doctor! He didn't come over, either. He said that sleep would be the best thing for her."

That was all Steve needed to hear. "I'll be there in half an hour," he said, hanging up on her protest.

But Mrs. Bellinger wasn't protesting when she admitted Steve into the Gunnerson house. In fact, she seemed relieved to see him. "Gail's awake," she said, her hand pressed against a palpably fluttering heart. "But she's just lying there, staring at the ceiling. She won't even talk to me about it."

"About what, exactly?"

"I tried to reach her doctor again, the *new* one." Mrs. Bellinger resisted using specific terminology when it came to Dr. Vanner, just as she never called the Mead Clinic by its name.

"Did you reach him?"

"No, only his answering service."

"Why didn't he come over the first time you called?"

"He said it wouldn't have done any good, that she'd probably sleep through the night. If only she had . . ."

"Tell me about this scare she had. What was it? Another noise in the house?"

"No," Mrs. Bellinger said, lowering her voice to befit the gravity of her statement. "Gail *saw* something to-night, at the door of her room. A ghost or a spirit, something like that."

Steve tried not to look worried.

"You mean it was like the last time? That mistake she made in the attic—seeing her mother's dress hanging from the beam."

"No," Mrs. Bellinger said. "This was different—this was much worse. She thinks there was someone at her door, someone who tried to come into her room. If you could have heard the way she screamed! When I finally got upstairs she was passed out cold."

"Did she descrbe this "Spirit'?"

"It was a woman, that's all she said—not her mother, no. At least that's what I could make out from what she was saying, none of it made much sense. She was talking out of her head, but now she's not talking at all. I looked in on her, and she was just lying there and wouldn't answer me . . ."

"Maybe she'll talk to me," Steve said, and headed for the stairway. He was halfway up by the time Mrs. Bellinger managed to move her bunioned feet to the landing and watch his progress toward the second floor.

He knocked on Gail's bedroom door first; there was no point in creating a secondary fright by an unannounced entrance. When there was no response to his light tapping, he let himself in.

Mrs. Bellinger's description had been accurate. But the moment Gail identified her new visitor, she let out a howl of unashamed misery that startled Steve and impelled him across the room like a short-distance runner. Even when she was in his arms her sobbing didn't subside, and he gave up useless questions for equally useless sounds of sympathy.

Eventually she was able to say a name.

"Helen," she said.

"Helen Malmquist? What about her?"

"She's dead," Gail told him. "Oh, Steve, she killed herself tonight; she cut her wrists!"

"My God. No wonder you're all shook up, having nightmares."

"No. You don't understand. I saw her, saw her body, and then I saw her *here*, at my door."

"Stop right there. Let's not talk about things you *saw,* let's talk about *dreams.*"

"No, no, that's what I'm trying to tell you, that's why it's so horrible! I didn't dream anything, I *saw* her, I could have reached out and touched her. It was Helen, just the way she looked, in her bathroom——"

"You say you actually saw the body? When was this?"

"Late this afternoon. I was at Dr. Vanner's, my usual appointment. Helen telephoned him at the offiice; she was threatening suicide, or hinting at it, at least. I volunteered to go over to her place and stay with her until he got rid of his next patient."

"So you went to Helen's apartment."

"Yes. Only I was too late! She'd already done it, Steve, she slashed her wrists, both of them. It was awful—there was blood all over the bathroom—running in the tub like water——"

"Gail, are you sure? You didn't get things mixed

up tonight, after you went to sleep? I know you're taking some medication—"

"I was there. I saw her. She was on the bath mat. She was wearing a negligee—a white-cotton thing—all stained with blood. Her arms were dripping blood, too . . . She was dead, but she came here. Helen came here, Steve."

She was shuddering so violently that he increased the strength of his embrace, wrapped his arms as tightly about her as if they were the cloth arms of a restraining camisole. The simile entered his mind like the point of a sharp needle.

"Gail, honey, you're confused now." He hated the way his own voice sounded, so measuredly calm that it was practically unctuous. "It's only natural that you would have a bad dream, a very vivid bad dream, after an episode like that, after seeing what you saw."

"But it wasn't, it wasn't! Look at me, Steve, look at my face!" He did. The heightened candlepower of her eyes, and suddenly leveled intensity of her voice, were more alarming than her words. "I saw Helen Malmquist tonight," she said. "She knocked at my bedroom door and woke me up. I got out of bed and opened the door and she was standing outside."

"No, baby . . ."

"She was standing there in her negligee, the same one she wore in the bathroom, all covered with blood. There was still blood on her wrists. I know because they were turned outwards, like this—" She demonstrated with her own arms. "She was dead, Steve, and yet she was here. She even spoke to me."

"And said what?"

"She said 'Come with me.' "

The clucking noise he made was a sound of annoyance.

"She said it, Steve! She held out her bloody arms to

me and tried to take me with her. That's what I saw just before I fainted. Thank God I fainted! But Helen was as real to me as you are—you have to believe that."

"Don't try so hard to make me *believe*," he said, pained. "Why do you want to convince me of something that both of us know can't be true?"

"Yes," she whispered. "That's what I've been telling myself. That there aren't any real ghosts, only in the mind. And when you see things you know can't exist, when they're as real as Helen was . . ."

"Stop it!"

Steve released her. Freed of his comforting embrace, she suddenly seemed free of her need for it. She fell back among her pillows again, her expression returning to one of empty resignation. If she had screamed suddenly, he could have been no less startled. But he also found himself jarred into the middle of a new idea that seemed to have the stunning validity of a new mathematical concept.

"Gail, please listen," he said. "I'm not going to argue with you, I'm going to agree with you. Did you hear what I said?"

She turned her head only slightly.

"I'm not trying to humor you. But something just occurred to me, about your friend Helen. How long have you known her, anyway?"

Her lips formed an answer he couldn't hear.

"You said it wasn't very long, didn't you? Just a few months, no lifelong friendship."

"No," she said.

"You met her at the Art League, isn't that right?"

Gail shook her head. "It was at a cafeteria. We shared a table. She had her art samples with her, and we got to talking."

"Then you really don't know much about her, do you?"

"What does it matter? She became my friend. And when I saw her that way tonight—"

"Maybe you didn't see what you think you saw. Maybe you didn't see Helen's body, maybe you saw Helen alive. Has that occured to you?"

Now the eyes were filled with bewilderment, which Steve preferred to the vacuum it replaced.

"What are you talking about?"

"Dead women don't knock on doors and carry on conversations, honey, not even in bloodstained negligees. I'm willing to consider the possibility that you *didn't* have a nightmare this evening, if *you'll* consider the possibility that you didn't see Helen Malmquist lying in any pool of blood."

"But I did! I know I did! I saw the razor blade she killed herself with—everything!"

"What if the 'everything' you saw was a stage setting?"

If nothing else, he was stirring the girl back to life.

"How could it be?"

"Why not? There are plenty of corpses on the stage, in the movies; bloody convincing ones, if you'll pardon the expression. What makes you think Helen might not have pulled a little Halloween prank on you? Out of season," he said wryly, "and maybe carried it just a little bit too far."

She was shaking her head again, with more animation.

"Think about it, honey, about what you actually saw in that apartment. Do you think you could have told the difference if that was ketchup in the bathtub, or red paint? You didn't touch the body, did you?"

"No. I didn't touch her. I couldn't. I turned and ran out as fast as I could—"

"Sure, that's what she would have counted on, plenty of shock value, enough to drive you out of the place with the conviction that she was really dead."

"Steve, you're wrong! It's not the first time that Helen tried to kill herself; I've seen the scars on her wrists! And there was a suicide note—"

"Maybe it was just a prop for Act One. All part of setting you up for Act Two—"

"You mean coming here."

"Yes, coming here. Getting into the house by whatever method she was using in the past." Gail bolted upright at this, and he put a steadying hand on her again. "That's what I'm really getting at, Gail, that this wasn't the first time that Helen played trick-or-treat with you. Maybe she's been doing it for months, making things go *bump* in the attic and elsewhere, rattling chains, doing God-knows-what-else to scare the daylights out of you . . ."

"But *why?*"

"I'll get to motive in a moment. Let's just talk about method. Suppose Helen had been interested in putting a real scare into you—what better way could there be than by making you see a ghost, her *own* ghost? She knew you were at Vanner's this evening, didn't she?"

"Yes. She knew what time I have my appointment."

"Okay. So she calls the doctor and pretends to be all upset, ready for the big plunge into eternity, figuring very well that you'll volunteer to go over there and hold her hand. But before you can get there, she's painted her hand blood-red. Get it?"

"No! Steve, there's no *reason* for anything like that—"

"What makes you so sure? I mean, are you really so sure that you can live in this world, and not have any enemies?"

"What would Helen have against me?"

"Maybe nothing, personally. Maybe she's just—well, a hired hand, okay?"

"Hired? Who would *hire* her to do such a dreadful thing?"

He tried not to make his hesitation too long. "Gail, there are lots of warped people in this world, sad to relate, and some of them may even be in positions with plenty of surface respectability. And when the stakes are very large, they may not be able to keep their moral principles intact—they may think they're justified in doing all kinds of weird and even criminal things—"

"I don't understand a word you're saying!"

"I'm not sure what I'm saying," he answered grimly, and not quite truthfully. "And maybe I have a very wet theory in mind. But there's one way to start checking it out."

"What's that?"

"By doing the obvious thing—finding out whether your friend Helen is alive or dead. *And* if she's your friend."

Squeezed into the back seat of a Nova cab inching its way from the East Side to the West, Steve asked himself the questions he would have spoken aloud in Gail Gunnerson's bedroom. If he was right about Helen Malmquist, then there were other villains in the piece, and the word "villain" was hard to placard under the broad open face of Saul Tedesco, even if hard logic placed it there. But what if his Uncle Saul wasn't the culprit? What if there were other officials at the Fiduciary Bank, not nearly as sanguine about the future of the Gunnerson account, and not nearly as ethical about preserving it, and being victims of their own greed, willing to make Gail a victim, too? Steve didn't know the exact value of the Gunnerson estate, but he had heard it referred to as "one of the ten largest personal fortunes in America," and weren't worse crimes committed for the sake of fewer dollars? Thirty silver ones, for instance? And another thought. What if Gail's coming-of-age did result in a change of banks, and therefore a subsequent audit? What if there was somebody who knew that any audit of her holdings would produce evidence of discrepancies, misuse of funds, even outright embezzlement? The Nova hit a pothole and bumped his head on the cab roof. He was almost grateful for the blow that interrupted his musing.

When the taxi turned up West End Avenue, the driver asked him for the exact location of the building. Steve couldn't oblige until his window framed a scene that made his heart constrict. There was a Police Department ambulance moving slowly and silently away from the curb in front of the brick pile on the corner of Eighty-fourth Street. Two patrol cars were double-parked nearby. Blue uniforms were interspersed among the fifty-odd spectators enjoying the street spectacular, but there was no sign of official bustle or hurry, no air of crisis. When he hopped out of the cab, Steve was the only one on the street who seemed agitated. When he recognized the sour-lemon face of Lt. Tom Baldridge, he was reluctant to flag his attention and hear the truth that was already self-evident, that cops don't bustle and ambulances don't sound their sirens for the already dead. But he stopped him anyway, and Baldridge, never pleased to see him, made his answer curt and definitive.

"Suicide," he said. "Woman named Helen Malmquist."

Eleven

Baldridge had warned him about the coffee, but Steve, familiar with the bitter black brew of half a dozen foreign news bureaus, didn't think that Precinct 20 could out-vile them. One sip and he knew better. Baldridge grinned as he took the cup from his hand and said: "Don't worry, I'm not trying to poison you. At least not until you ask your second question."

"I'm still not satisfied with my first answer."

The lieutenant shrugged. "We don't dig that deep into the *why* of a suicide, Mr. Tyner. Especially when we have documented evidence of emotional troubles. You knew this Helen Malmquist was undergoing psychiatric treatments?"

"Vanner isn't just a psychiatrist. He's also a psychoanalyst."

"You want to argue the difference, pick a fight with the medical boys, not me."

"No," Steve said glumly, "I don't want to argue with anyone. And I know the girl had a history of depression. That's what I heard, anyway."

"From our mutual friend, Miss Gunnerson?"

"I didn't come here to talk about her."

"Didn't you? I thought maybe the lady asked you to make the inquiry. Since she was pretty close to the deceased at one time—am I right?" Baldridge, eyes

111

level with Steve, picked up the rejected coffee mug and
sipped without so much as a grimace.

"Okay, I'm curious because of Miss Gunnerson. And
for my own sake. I knew Helen Malmquist, too."

"Good. Then you probably knew this was her second attempt at cutting her wrists. The first one was
maybe five, six years ago, less effective, obviously. In
addition to all that, we have a voluntary statement
made by a man named Larry Rosenbaum. Are you
familiar with him?"

"No," Steve said.

"He was Helen Malmquist's sometime boyfriend, the
last one in her life, and we sort of get the picture that
she took him a little more seriously than he took her.
Then of course there's her suicide note. In case that's
your *second* question, Mr. Tyner, we don't have the
slightest doubt about its authenticity."

"That *wasn't* going to be my second question," Steve
said. "I'm not saying that Helen Malmquist wasn't a
suicide, I'm just trying to learn if there were things
about the woman that came out of your investigation,
things we didn't know before."

"Let's say something did. What would be the point
of telling you about it?"

"Lieutenant, you know I'm a licensed investigator,
and you were willing to cooperate with me in the
past."

"About an entirely different matter, yes. Just because
the Malmquist woman was a *friend* of Gail Gunnerson,
that doesn't seem to justify all the time you're taking
up." When Steve didn't answer, Baldridge sighed and
said: "Okay, I'll tell you what little I know. Miss
Malmquist doesn't have any family except for an aunt
who lives in Seattle who hasn't laid eyes on her niece
since she was an infant. She's lived in three cities that
we know about after her family left the Northwest

when she was a kid—L.A., Phoenix, and New York. We think she was living with some guy in Phoenix who left her; that's when she must have done the first job on her wrists. She collected some insurance money from her father's death, and went abroad, stayed there about eighteen months, went to a couple of art schools, one in Paris, one in Switzerland. Then she came back to New York and stayed here, enrolled in the Art League, signed up for a little couch time, and finally —ended up with that razor blade in her hand."

Flatly, Steve said: "That's how she did it, then? A razor blade?"

"She was neat about it, anyway. You wouldn't think she was a neat type, judging from all the dirty dishes in the sink, but she made sure the mess was kept to a minimum."

"Can you describe it for me? I mean, how you found her, exactly?"

Baldridge narrowed his eyes. "Why? What's so important about it?"

"I'd just like to know. Call it morbid curiosity. Just tell me this one thing and I'll stop bothering you."

"All right," Baldridge said. "She killed herself in the bathroom. She put on a cotton negligee with no sleeves, and sat down on the bath mat with a single-edge blade. She started the water running and then slashed both her wrists. When she passed out, her head hit the edge of the tub. After a while, she died."

He picked up the coffee cup and finished it down to the bitter dregs. When he placed it back on the table, Steve looked into the cup and watched a streak of muddy black grounds slide down toward the bottom. He thought it was the most depressing sight he had ever seen in his life.

When he telephoned the Gunnerson house from the

pay phone on the corner, he was angered when he learned from Mrs. Bellinger that Gail was in bed.

"Whose idea was that? What the hell good is lying in bed going to do her; she hasn't got the measles! She'll just get more depressed in that damned room!"

Mrs. Bellinger was offended. "It wasn't my idea, it was her *doctor's*."

"You mean Vanner?"

"Yes, the new one. She won't let me call Dr. Yost, her medical doctor. She says there's nothing he can do for her."

"Buzz her room. Let me speak to her."

"She told me she wouldn't take any calls."

"I don't care what she told you," Steve said threateningly. "I want to talk to Gail. I want to get her out of that miserable bed and on her feet!"

"I'm sorry, I just can't do that, I can't go against doctor's orders!"

Steve swore aloud, but hung up in time to permit Mrs. Bellinger to think he was merely invoking the name of some maternal ancestor. Then he dialed Vanner's office, and as he expected, got the doctor's answering service.

"I know, I know, the doctor has office hours, and he won't be interrupted. Only I have to speak to him right away, and I won't be at this number very long."

Vanner finally called him fifteen minutes later. Steve bristled at his first remark.

"Well, what's so urgent?"

"Do you know where this phone booth is?" Steve said harshly. "Just outside of Precinct 20 of the New York Police Department."

Dryly: "Been arrested, Mr. Tyner? Call a lawyer, not a doctor."

"I've been down here talking about Helen Malmquist's suicide."

"Why? What concern is it of yours?"

"I understand the police have already discussed it with you."

"Of course they have. Helen was my patient. I told them all I thought they needed to know about her problems. I hardly see what you could contribute."

"You told them all about Helen. But what about your other patient? Gail Gunnerson?"

"I don't know what you mean."

"You never informed the police that Gail went to Helen Malmquist's apartment, did you? That *she* was the one who actually discovered the body, not you."

There was a moment of dead air.

"I saw no need to involve Gail in this business. I made one mistake by allowing her to go to that apartment in place of myself. I refused to compound my error by having her bothered by the police."

"Then what she told me is true," Steve said. "That she found Helen in the bathroom."

"Yes, it's true. It's regrettable, of course. As you know, Gail is only too susceptible to fears, all kinds of fears. Seeing what she did—well, it might affect the progress of her therapy, no doubt about that."

"Have you seen her since?"

"No. The last time I saw Gail was at Helen's place. I advised her to go home, to stay in bed and remain as calm as possible."

"She took the advice pretty seriously. She's still in bed. Has been for the past twenty-four hours."

"So I understand. I spoke to her by phone several times. I don't think the rest is doing her any harm."

"You don't."

"No."

"Has it occurred to you that it might not be doing her any good, either? Have you thought of paying a house call to find out for yourself?"

"We discussed an office appointment for the early part of next week, if she's up to it."

"Look," Steve said sourly, "you know what I'm really asking about, don't you?"

"No, I'm afraid I don't."

"I'm asking about what happened to Gail *after* Helen Malmquist did herself in. I'm sure she must have told you about it by now, about seeing Helen come back from the dead."

In the pause that followed, Steve fervently wished for the rapid development of phonovision. All he could do was imagine Vanner's reaction from the thin vibrations of his reply.

"No," the doctor said. "She hasn't told me anything about a nightmare."

"Correction," Steve said. "Not nightmare. The word is hallucination—or worse. That's the real reason she's staying under the covers. She's hiding from whatever it is that makes people see ghosts coming through their door."

"I'm sorry. I don't think we're on the same wavelength."

"I'm telling you that Gail Gunnerson thinks she's coming apart, that the thread is winding off the spool and there's no way to stop it! The girl needs help and she needs it now!"

"I'll do what I can," Vanner said stiffly. "But I have to proceed the way I think best. And if you think this denotes a lack of caring about my patient, Mr. Tyner, you're very wrong. There's no one who cares more about what happens to Gail Gunnerson than I do, no one in the world, including yourself."

Steve had to admit: he said it with feeling.

Gail was still in her bedroom when Steve called at the Gunnerson house later that afternoon. She was sitting on the chair beside her bed, wearing a robe with sunny daffodils all over it. Progress, Steve thought. Except that he couldn't help noticing that the flowery prettiness of the robe contrasted unbecomingly with her colorless skin and puffy eyes.

"You're looking better," he said gallantly.

"You're not lying any better," she answered. "What did you do today?"

"Well, isn't this domestic." He smiled. "I tell you what I did at the office, and you tell me what you're cooking for supper."

"Speaking of supper—if you'd like to stay, Mrs. Bellinger said she's made enough stew for an army."

"Will you come downstairs and join us?"

"No. I'll have a tray up here. Much as I hate to have that poor woman climb those stairs."

"I can solve the problem. I'll have my stew on a tray, too, and I'll bring up *both* our suppers. How does that grab you?"

"All right," Gail said flatly.

"Not thrilled at the prospect, evidently."

" 'Not thrilled at the prospect,' " she repeated. "Yes. That's a very good description of how I feel right now. About supper tonight, and breakfast tomorrow, and all the meals after that." She looked up at him. "I wonder what kind of meals they serve in *those* places. Soups, probably, and stews, too, most likely. Maybe that's what Mrs. Bellinger is trying to do, get me used to that kind of food."

"I don't get the joke."

"I mean they can't very well give us steaks and roast beef or anything else you have to cut with a knife. Maybe not even forks. They'd be afraid to do that. We might start carving up each other, all us loonies—"

"Now I *do* get the joke," Steve said, frowning. "Only it's not very funny."

"I'm not trying to amuse you. Maybe I'm trying to warn you."

"About what?"

"About me. About being mixed up with me. Having supper on the same tray, even. Who knows? It might be catching, this disease of mine."

"I knew it," Steve said. "I knew you'd get yourself worked up into a state of depression if you stayed in this room. I told your great Dr. Vanner that."

"You spoke to him?"

"Yes, this afternoon. I wanted to find out what his opinion was, about this nightmare you had."

Gail said: "I haven't told him about it. About seeing Helen."

"I know you haven't. And I think you should as soon as possible. I think you need someone with a little more authority than me to convince you that it wasn't as serious as you seem to think. That one hallucination isn't enough to put you in a nut-house dining room without knives or forks . . ."

Something crackled in the bedroom. It surprised Steve, but Gail seemed to recognize the source. She rose wearily and went to the nightstand of her bed. Sitting next to a porcelain ballerina poised crookedly on a music-box base was a small brown instrument with a fabric grill. Gail turned a knob and said: "Yes, Mrs. Bellinger?"

"There's some mail for you, honey."

"At this hour?"

"It's Special Delivery. A big envelope. Do you want me to bring it upstairs?"

"Can you tell where it came from?"

"London, the postmark says."

Gail looked at Steve, who volunteered quickly. "I'll

get it. Tell Mrs. Bellinger to keep her corn plasters on."

Rebounding up the stairs with the manila envelope in hand, he studied the markings but saw no return address, only a cluster of regal stamps and the dated postmark. Judging from the shifting weight of it, there were evidently several enclosures.

They turned out to be letters. The neatly slitted envelopes were loosely bound in ribbon, and bore U.S. postage stamps. Even without being a philatelist, Steve could discern that they were at least of twenty years vintage.

"What are they?" he said. "Who sent them?"

"They're all from my father." She shuffled through them with some bewilderment. "They're letters written by my father to his brother in London. Every one of them is addressed to Gilbert Swann, 21, Fulham Road."

"Who sent them to you? Is there a note attached?"

"There's a note, but it's not addressed to me. It just says: 'Estate of Gilbert Swann, Esq. Forwarded by Mr. Spyker, Tremont, Tushingham and Spyker, London.' "

"Sounds like a law firm."

"I suppose."

"They must have found the letters among your uncle's personal effects. And since you were the only remaining relative, I guess they decided they should be yours."

"Yes," Gail said, slipping one of the sheets out of the envelope with no regard for chronological order. She scanned the typewritten lines swiftly, but then looked at Steve with troubled eyes before reaching the bottom of the page. "I don't feel right reading this. I know they're my own father's letters, but it still seems like an invasion of privacy."

"I wouldn't think of it that way," Steve said gently, feeling a sense of relief at this timely distraction. "When someone dies, their letters become property. In this case, your property. As Tremont, Tushingham and Spyker." Grinning. "Great names, those English law firms."

She was reading the second page.

"He's writing about my mother!"

Steve wasn't so sure now that the distraction was welcome. "What's the date on the letter?"

"February 14, 1953."

"Check the other dates. You might want to read them in the correct sequence."

"Yes," Gail said, beginning to sort them in her lap. "The earliest seems to be in 1952, December the fourth." She opened the letter; the stationery was still white and crisp. Steve sneaked a look at the neatly typed salutation. "Dear Gil," it read, "I'm sorry to say that Cressie's illness makes a trip abroad—" That was all he could see; he assumed that the next word would be something like "impossible." Denied the reading privilege, he read Gail's expression instead. She went straight through the letter to its final paragraph, and Steve saw something "impossible" happen to her face; it grew even paler than it had been before.

"What is it? What does the letter say?" She didn't reply. "Something about your mother's illness?"

"It must have been just the beginning of it, Steve; it's awful!"

"What are you talking about? From what I understand, your mother was perfectly fine until your father got himself shot up in Korea. That's when she started going to pieces."

Gail shook her head, and then, as if to force him into understanding, shoved the letter into his hand. He read it through while she opened still another envelope.

    Dear Gil,

I'm sorry to say that Cressie's illness makes a trip abroad impossible before I enter military service. The request I have from Col. Siefert asks me to report to him in Washington on 3/5/53 and I simply can't take the chance that C. will be well enough to travel in time to make the journey worth the trouble. Thank you for the invitation anyway and for your good wishes for her speedy recovery. One which hasn't come our way, as you might gather. What really worries me, Gilly, and please don't mention this to anyone—and don't talk about it in your own letters to me, because you know how households full of servants, etc. can be, altogether too much curiosity about letters and things. I once caught a maid named Normalie (believe that name?) steaming open an envelope over a teakettle in the kitchen, hoping there'd be money in it, I suppose, or juicy gossip. As I recall there was nothing but a tailor's bill. At any rate, make no mention of anything I tell you about this, but Cressie did *not* have a bad case of pneumonia last month, even if that was the official diagnosis we released to the world at large. Actually, the fever she had was relatively mild and didn't last more than twenty-four hours, but the reason Dr. Halevy kept her in bed for such a long period of time was what he called a touch of "brain fever." To be honest, Gil, I don't know if there's any such thing or if it isn't some kind of mid-Victorian euphemism they cooked up to explain the "vapors" or little nervous breakdowns our ancestors were constantly having in that impossible society. At any rate, that's what Dr.

Halevy called it, and told me not to worry too much, that Cressie is just high-strung, and that the prospect of my entering the Army and maybe getting my head shot off in some battlefield has upset her. I know for a fact that she *is* upset about my applying for the commission, but I've told her a hundred times that Siefert has asked me to be in his personal command the the old boy isn't going to get within hearing range of a battle unless he's changed completely since we knew him at the Academy. Actually, the Colonel's getting very deaf, judging from my last phone call to him. Lately, I've almost wished that Cressie was hard-of-hearing, too, because that's been her main problem, and that's what worries me so much. She's hearing things, strange noises, thumps and bumps all over the house every night, waking me up two or three times, convinced that we have burglars upstairs and down. She's normal enough in the daytime, but the minute the sun goes I know she's going to behave exactly the same way. To be honest, I've started to dread the coming of darkness. I never get a full night's sleep, and you know how much I need my ten hours—remember my telling you what a wreck I was when Gail was born, and that damned colic kept her crying at all hours. Of course the baby nurse was there, but Cressie woke up too whenever she heard that pitiful wail—anyway, in case you're wondering, Mrs. B. is taking care of Gail through this miserable time which I hope won't last very long. That and this miserable war or police action or whatever the hell it is that's killing people over in that funny country that half of us never even heard of before 1950. When it's over, you can be sure that we'll take you up on the offer to visit you and Piers in London. Write soon, even if you have to use one of your quill pens.

Regards,
Teddy

Gail had finished her letter first. She didn't open a third; she just stared at Steve, waiting for his comment.

"Okay," he said. "So your mother heard some noises, too. If you think there's any parallel in that, you're right. I told you that this house must be a natural noisemaker. Full of squeaks and groans, creaking shutters and floorboards, mice playing Little League baseball in the walls . . ."

"My *father* didn't hear those noises, Steve. Only my mother. She was the only one. Just like *I'm* the only one."

"He was a sound sleeper, obviously; didn't you read what he says about getting his ten hours? The only thing that woke him up at night, probably, was your mother shaking him. And I'll bet your Mrs. Bellinger is just as impervious."

For answer, she handed him the second letter.

"Read that," Gail said.

Steve checked the date. April 9, 1953. It was postmarked from Washington D.C.

Dear Gil,

Sorry it's been so long since I've written, but judging from the length of time since your last letter, I can only assume that you didn't find the quill pen necessary to turn you into any kind of decent correspondent. Sorry if the joke isn't very funny but I'm not in the mood for humor these days considering the state of Cressie's health. I might as well tell you right off that she's under the care of a psychiatrist, actually an Army officer who left a very good practice in Philadelphia; name of Vogel. Cressie resisted the idea of seeing him; in fact, there was a great deal of subterfuge employed in order to make it possible for her to be examined by the man. He's one of these very cautious types that won't make swift judgments, but he was candid with me and said that he did detect signs of what he called a schizoid personality in Cressie. From what I gather there's a kind of dissociation taking place, please don't ask me to explain the way or how of it. He speculated that her auditory hallucinations have some connection with the fears of her childhood, evidently fears of intrusion, invasion, prowlers and marauders entering her house . . . Although he said a few troubling things about "house" being an inexact word in this context . . .

Steve lowered the letter and made a grumbling sound. "Look, I'm not sure this is such a great idea, this reading session. Especially if you're going to take this stuff more literally than you should."

"What could be more literal?" Gail said. "This is about *her,* Steve, about my mother. The truth about her, things I never even knew before."

"Maybe you're better off not knowing them."

But she began the third letter, and her stricken expression caused Steve to drop to one knee and read it over her shoulder.

It was dated June 22, 1953, and still postmarked Washington, D.C.

Dear Gil,
By now, of course, I expect you've heard about the sudden death of Col. Siefert. It was a great shock to all of us, and in case you're wondering, I

believe that it will make a difference in my status here. In fact, the possibility of active service now seems greater than ever, and frankly I don't know whether my circumstances would be bettered or worsened by being shipped overseas. I suppose I could defer any such action if I wished to plead a hardship case, and I'm referring specifically to Cressie, whose illness has gotten worse despite the therapy of Dr. Vogel, who himself may be leaving Washington for another assignment shortly. He may be glad of it, since he has been unable to cope with the developing schizophrenia of my wife, whose symptoms now include (I'm quoting from a list Dr. V. gave me): depersonalization, derealization, nihilistic delusions, delusions of persecution, visual hallucination. The last describes a horrible episode that I've been unwilling to tell anyone, and writing you at least affords me the relief of describing this nightmarish business. It occurred within twenty-four hours of the Colonel's heart attack, and although Siefert was a frequent visitor to our apartment, I would hardly say that I expected his death to affect Cressie deeply. But it seems to have done exactly that, because in the middle of the night, she began to scream, and I mean scream at the top of her lungs, incessantly; nothing I could do would make her stop. She swore to me that Colonel Siefert was in the house, that he was sitting downstairs in the living room, and wouldn't leave until Cressie herself went down to be with him, until she herself left the house with his "spirit." I know how terribly mad this sounds, Gilly, but this is exactly what occurred, and you can imagine how shocking it was for me. Even worse to report, she has clung to this same delusion, to the notion that old Colonel had come back to take her with him, to this very moment, and

I confess to a desire for escape from her problems
and the ones she has created for me, selfish as that
may sound . . .

"It's me," Gail said to Steve.

He put his hand out to touch her, and she avoided
it almost in revulsion.

"Please don't try to comfort me," Gail said. "Just try
to understand me. Try to take this thing for what it is,
Steve, without fooling either one of us. Don't you see
what these letters show? My mother started to go mad
before my father was killed; it wasn't just an attack of
melancholia, it was something deeper, much deeper,
so deep that it was carried in her genes."

"You don't know anything of the kind!"

"Her madness was just like mine, and it ended up
with them deciding to put her away. But she stopped
that by killing herself. That's the only reason she
stayed out of an asylum, Steve, because she took her
life!"

"Stop making yourself an expert! Ask your doctor,
for Pete's sake—stop making your own diagnoses!"

"They're going to put me away, just like they would
have done to her. You know that as well as I do."

"They don't just 'put people away,'" Steve said sav-
agely. "They can just *commit* people unless they've
been proved to be a danger to themselves or others,
or if some member of their family can prove that their
and the community's interests would be best served by
forcible treatment."

"You sound as if you've looked this up."

"At least I know the law in this state about such
things, a little bit of it, anyway."

"So do I," Gail said flatly. "I've looked it up, too,

Steve. And I know that there *are* people with enough authority to put me in one of those places, people like the executors of my trust, for instance. Since they're the closest people I have in the world."

"That's nonsense. The *Bank* isn't going to put you into an institution."

"The trustees could start proceedings and make it happen. Nothing can stop them if they proved their case, Steve—don't you realize that?"

"They're not your *kin*."

"But I don't have anyone else. Anyone who could stand up for me in a legal battle. My parents are dead, my uncle is dead. Who's going to stand up for me, Steve—Mrs. Bellinger? Dr. Vanner, Dr. Yost?"

"How about me?"

"You don't know what you're saying."

"Sure, I know. You think I haven't thought about it? And *not* because of any threat to slap you into a padded cell."

"What do you mean?"

"I mean that if you had a husband to stand up for you, nobody could hurt you. That's what I'm proposing. God knows I didn't mean it to be done this way, but why the hell don't you just marry me?"

Twelve

He liked the look of his gloved hands on the steering wheel. It was the only sartorial habit he adopted from his father. For some reason, he associated dove-gray gloves with wealth, the best kind of wealth, employed with a casual grace approaching indifference. That was the kind of millionaire he planned to be. The car he would drive then would be no bigger than the rented compact he was in now. But it wouldn't be stamped out of a Detroit cookie cutter; it would be German, some limited edition model, owner-driven. If he ever did hire a chauffeur, he would sit beside him democratically and talk about the weather. He would build no mansions. He would buy or lease some well-established homes and villas of modest size. He planned no yachts, no lavish entertainments, no high-priced mistresses. There would be nothing ostentatious about the way he would spend Gail Gunnerson's money.

The prospects rolled before his eyes more clearly than the city streets funneling into his windshield. There was only one thing that troubled him about the imagined future. For a time certain doors would be closed to him. (When the word "doors" entered his head, he grimaced.) He would have to stay out of the United States, that was certain. Even after the hairy mask he wore had been shaved away, there was risk of recognition. It wasn't very great, as risks go. He had skillfully avoided lengthy face-to-face encounters. He had made no friends or even casual acquaintances. Yes, there was a time when he had to beard the police (that word made him smile), but the encounter was brief; he felt sure that the lieutenant who queried him about poor Helen Malmquist had been left with no strong impression of his features beyond the obvious: the heavy-framed eyeglasses, the neat reddish mustache and luxuriant beard; take them away and what was left? No, he had no real concerns about the policeman (what was his name again? something bald). His only real concern was Steve Tyner, the Lothario who had suddenly attached himself to Gail. Problem there, maybe. (He frowned into the car's rear-view mirror as if expecting to see Steve's car tailing him.) No, it would be best to be cautious. He would return to Europe as soon as IT had been accomplished. He would check himself into that hospital in Vienna, complaining of violent headaches; he would be unable to give the admissions clerk any clear identification. It wouldn't take long for the learned physicans (their apperceptions already waist-deep in the murky waters of psychoanalysis) to reach the conclusion that he was the sorry victim of circumscribed amnesia, that some head injury or serious trauma had short-circuited his memory of the past six months. And then the answers would come. If they were slow arriving at them, he would help. He would cry out in the night about falling clouds of snow. He would shiver and tremble and shake with cold on warm summer evenings. And soon the deduction would be made. Piers Swann is alive. Piers Swann is alive and well and will soon be living in luxury. Perhaps the auditors and bank executors and probate courts would have finished their task by then. Perhaps, when some fine ruddy-faced Viennese doctor informed Piers of his true identity, he would lock his hands behind his back and add: "And you are a rich man, Mr. Swann, a very rich man . . ."

He chuckled at the image of the doctor. He was sure he would look very much like Professor Eckstein at the University of Vienna, whose courses in psycho-analytic theory he had audited for almost a year. Eckstein would never know how grateful he was to him. Or to Ludovic, for that matter, the student he had met at the Balkan Grill, who told him, between czardas and slivovitzes, how impressed the *Madchen* were when they learned you were a disciple of Freud and Adler; perhaps stimulated by the notion that you knew secret things about sexuality.

It was Ludovic who showed him 19 Berggasse, where Freud had lived and worked; Ludovic who gave him the books to read and the vocabulary to be absorbed; and when his pupil had learned his lessons well, it was Ludovic who had presented him with the diploma engraved in the name of Sigmund Fraud. Piers had been more intrigued than amused because the certifi-cate itself was so obviously authentic in everything but the name. Ludovic, it seemed, had a friend who worked for a printing concern which specialized in such grand documents, and with typical Viennese *Schlamperei* carelessly disposed of its less than perfect copies. The one that Piers obtained for his later pur-poses was too lightly inked for the taste of the per-fectionist printer; otherwise it was flawless. Piers had no difficulty adding the name in the proper place (*Joel* because he liked the name; *Vanner* because he saw it on a bakery truck). He had always been re-markably adept with a pen; if other avenues hadn't opened up to him, he might well have become a master forger. He smiled, thinking of the letters he had just written, and how much pleasure he had taken in them: not so much with the calligraphy, but with the composition. He had done more than imitate Theodore Gunnerson's handwriting; he had assimilated the writing style he had discovered in the original letters. He had destroyed those, saving only the envelopes in which they had arrived at 21, Fulham Road. Looking admiringly at his gray-gloved hands on the wheel, he decided that someone so multi-talented deserved to be rich.

"Dr. Vanner!"

He had become so accustomed to thinking himself Piers Swann again that he almost failed to respond properly to the sound of his new name. He paused at the landing of the Gunnerson stairway, one gray-gloved hand on the newel post, and turned to look at Steve Tyner. Steve was holding a tray; the dinner plates steamed richly.

"I didn't know you were here, Mr. Tyner."

"I'm here," Steve said. "I was just going to bring Gail some supper."

"Why don't I take it to her? I can talk to her while she eats."

"I've got a better idea," Steve said. "Why don't you and I talk first? Mrs. Bellinger——" He turned to the housekeeper behind him. "Could you keep these warm for a few minutes while I talk to the doctor?"

"Yes, of course," Mrs. Bellinger said. She took the tray from him and bore it toward the kitchen, trailing vapor like a steamboat. Steve nodded toward the parlor and Vanner shrugged and followed him, peeling off his gloves as he went. "You were very eager for me to see Miss Gunnerson," he said dryly. "But now that I'm here, you prefer to chat."

"I thought I could prepare you," Steve said, flopping

into a wing chair. "Things have changed upstairs since I spoke to you this afternoon."

"For better or worse?"

"A little of both. Gail's still convinced that she's a prime candidate for a funny coat. Maybe I could have talked her out of it, but then those letters arrived."

"Letters?"

"Some correspondence between her father and his brother, concerning her mother's health. They were forwarded here by some law firm in London. Their timing couldn't have been worse."

"I'm not following you," Vanner said, taking a seat himself and slapping his gloves impatiently into his lap.

"It seemed to give her a different picture of her mother's emotional problems. Gail always believed—always *wanted* to believe—that the only reason her mother went bonkers was because of her father's death. I think it was vital for her to believe that, if you know what I mean."

"I see you've got both feet in my territory again."

"You *do* know what I mean. It was necessary for Gail to understand what made her mother go off the rails. She didn't want to think it was anything organic. No, that's not the operative word. I mean anything . . . hereditary."

"And how would these letters indicate that?"

"They don't prove anything of the kind, they just make it evident that there was something wrong with her mother long before her suicide. Even before her father went into the Army. You don't look very surprised," Steve said.

"Why should I be?" Vanner shrugged. "I haven't been treating Gail's mother posthumously. I never took her word for it that her mother went mad because she lost her husband. Callous as it may sound, few women do."

"But didn't you always suppose it was depression that drove her to suicide?"

"People aren't usually laughing and giggling when they hang themselves." Vanner stood up; his gloves plopped softly on the carpet. "Look, my friend. I came to see my patient, and not to have a seminar on abnormal psychology."

"I'm asking your opinion, dammit!" Steve said. "That girl up there is starting to believe she *has* to go nuts because her mother did, that there's something in her genes or her blood that absolutely has it all foreordained, and I want you to tell her how wrong she is!"

"Because she's wrong, or because you think it's best to humor her?"

"Do you mean she might be *right?*"

Vanner's sigh was one of professional fatigue. "You'd be amazed how confused opinions are about inherited insanity."

"What *are* the opinions? About schizophrenia, for instance? Can you *inherit* schizophrenia, the way you can diabetes?"

"Some people think so. The chance of *anyone* becoming schizophrenic is about fifty to one. But for the child of a schizophrenic parent—it's less than ten to one. When both parents have a history; try *two* to one."

"Her father seems to have been okay," Steve said. The tone was almost wistful.

"I'm not taking sides on the issue," Vanner said generously. "There's also a school of thought which says those figures are perfectly compatible with the belief that schizophrenia is preconditioned by environment. A disturbed parent is a very important part of any kid's environment, wouldn't you say?"

Steve was shaking his head. It wasn't a negative sign; he just wanted to rattle his brains into clarity.

"You've got to ease her mind. You've got to tell Gail that nobody's going to put her into an institution. If she goes on thinking that way, she's liable to do anything."

"Describe 'anything.' "

"I'd rather not."

Vanner retrieved his gloves. He slapped them against the chair to remove the carpet dust, and then turned to leave the room. He was halfway out when Steve said: "Would you let them commit her?"

Vanner did a slow turn. "What was that you said?"

"Would you be on their side if they brought commitment proceedings against Gail? The law requires two physicians; you'd be the logical choice for one of them, although it doesn't say anyplace that the doctors have to be psychiatrists."

"Who is this mysterious 'they' you're talking about?"

"You know as well as I do."

"Ah," Vanner said. "The Bank."

"They're what you'd call the 'interested party,' " Steve said, every word making his back teeth ache. "Since Gail has no other family, they're legally entitled to petition for a hearing. They could present their evidence in court, they could try to prove that Gail is a danger to herself and a menace to her own money. Even if they didn't succeed, can you imagine what it would do to Gail, waiting to hear the worst?"

"Is that the 'anything' you were referring to?"

"Why do we have to play word games? You know I'm talking about suicide. Now answer my question." The last part of his statement came out more truculent than Steve intended. He could see Vanner bristling, and he had the bristles to do it with.

"You're quite a case of divided personality yourself," he said, a muscle leaping in his jaw. "You're not sure where *you* stand in this business, since you work for the Bank."

"I know exactly where I'm going to stand," Steve said. "That's what I wanted to tell you. I'm going to stand on Gail's right and say the magic words."

"What words?"

" 'I do.' "

He was pleased to see Vanner's eyes widen.

"Are you talking about marriage?"

"The only reason Gail is defenseless is that she doesn't have a relative to stand between her and the Bank. And I'm *not* saying that the Fiduciary is out to frame her into an institution; it's nothing like that, it never was. They had plenty of good reason to worry about her mental stability, and their concern was legitimate. I know that for a fact."

"Yes, I'm sure they're all terribly nice people," Vanner said dryly. "Which is why you want to marry Gail Gunnerson and protect her from their concern."

"The fact that I'll be able to short-circuit any insanity proceeding is only incidental. I just don't want to spend my honeymoon in a padded room. Although, come to think of it, that might be interesting."

Unamused: "Have you already proposed to her?"

"Yes."

"Did she accept?"

"Not yet. She thinks the way you do. That I'm marrying her for altruistic reasons. Actually, I'm marrying her for her money."

"Many a truth is told in jest." Joel Vanner smiled. Then he went upstairs. Steve followed him into the hallway, but not in time to see the smile vanish and his mouth turn to iron.

"Go ahead and cry if you like," he told her. "You've cried in front of me before."

"I don't feel like crying. I can't. Crying is something you do to get sympathy, even from yourself."

"Such a wise remark," Vanner said, and stroked a lock of hair out of her eyes the way he might have done for a child. "But a little too glib, if you want my opinion."

"But it's true," Gail said. "I've noticed that, all my life. When something is really wrong, when I'm really *afraid*, there isn't any relief in crying. My tear ducts don't seem to function."

"I really should take notes." He chuckled. "I'm learning so many things about my own profession this evening."

"Is Steve still here? He said he was going down to get our supper."

"Yes, he's still here, and supper will be forthcoming. But I wanted to see you first. Are you starving, or do you have some time for me?"

"I'm not starving. I'm not hungry in the least. Fear is wonderful for the waistline, isn't it?"

"And what are you afraid of, exactly?"

"Of myself, of course," Gail said. "Of what myself is going to do to me. I've been lying here wondering if my hands are going to pay any more attention to my brain. If my legs might decide to revolt against my arms. What would happen, Doctor? I mean, if the different parts of us went to war against each other?"

"All people are divided into three parts," Vanner said lightly. "Like Gaul."

"I know," she said, turning her face into the cooler side of her pillow. "Id, Ego, and Superego. The Three

Marx Brothers. No wonder we're such comical creatures."

"Which one is the Id?"

"Harpo, of course. The one who says nothing and chases girls." When he laughed, she turned to look at him with her eyes oddly lit from within. "I'm doing it now," she said. "I'm doing exactly what Father said *she* did."

" 'She' meaning your mother?"

"It was in the last letter. But you don't know about the letters, do you?"

"Steve Tyner mentioned something. I didn't see why it was so terribly important."

"You'll have to read them," Gail said. "You'll have to read them and see. Like the last one. About Mother's little jokes, her little outlandish remarks, half of them without any sense. But she would smile and laugh as if they struck her as terribly amusing. Father said that was how he became convinced that she was losing her mind. Not because of any hysterical outbursts, running naked in the streets, nothing like that. Just the constant, meaningless smile on her face, the sad funny little sayings . . ."

"It's not uncommon," Vanner said. "Many disturbed people become like children, looking for approval for their bright sayings. I've seen them in institutions." He tried to cut the word short, but failed.

"My mother never went into an institution. You knew that, didn't you?"

"Yes."

"She dreaded that idea more than the idea of death."

"She probably had some strong misconceptions about them. She probably visualized something along the lines of the old Bedlam."

"Did they call it Bedlam because it was noisy, or did the word come later? Was it a place full of beds?"

"The word came from the place. And it had nothing to do with beds. It was merely the shortened version of Bethlehem. Bethlehem Royal Hospital, the first asylum in England."

"We had relatives in England," Gail said thickly. "But you know about that, of course. Why am I telling you things you already know?"

"It's the pill I just gave you." Vanner smiled. "It's making you drowsy."

"My voice sounds far away. Is this the pill ventriloquists take to make their voice sound far away?"

"Gail, I think we should talk seriously about what happened to you. I think it's time that we faced the question directly and determined what has to be done."

"To be done," she repeated flatly. "To be done. It sounds so much like a drum roll, doesn't it? Very ominous sort of drum roll. To be done. To be done."

"Gail—"

"I'm sorry. I'm sorry," she said, reaching out and grasping his hand. "I know I'm acting silly. The truth is, I shouldn't have let you give me *another* one of those pills—I've already taken one more than I should have, one more than you told me to take. But it's helped me, it really has. What's in those pills, Doctor, concentrate of Martini?"

Vanner frowned and said: "We have some serious decisions to make, Gail, and they can't wait. If we delay, those decisions could be taken out of our hands."

"Mrs. Bellinger has made stew," Gail said. "Enough for an army. Would you like to enlist, Doctor?"

"This latest hallucination of yours can't simply be ignored. It's indicative of a serious symptom formation. It's forcing me to revise my diagnosis, Gail. Much as I've wanted to deny that the illness was progressive in nature, the facts are staring us both in the face."

He realized she wasn't listening, and Vanner cursed his haste in dropping still another tranquilizing dose into her bloodstream. He tilted her chin upward and saw that the damned-fool girl was actually smiling.

"Gail, I have to make you realize how serious things have become."

"Yes," she said. "I really think he was serious."

"He?"

"Steve. I really think he meant it. He asked me to marry him, or did I tell you that? And you know—something? I can't remember what I said to him. Yes or no. I'm sure I didn't say no, did I? Did he mention anything to you?"

"He mentioned it," Vanner said coldly. "However, there was no question in my mind whether he was 'serious' or not. He wasn't. He seems to have some misguided notion that marriage would be some kind of panacea for all your problems. Far from it. Marriage would create more problems."

"What did you say?"

The faint smile was gone, to Vanner's gratification. "I said that it wasn't a real proposal, Gail. I'm sorry."

"But it was! I heard him! Right in this room."

"No," Vanner said, shaking his head slowly. "I'm afraid that it was simply one more tactic on Mr. Tyner's part. And one that I deeply regret he used."

"Tactic? What sort of word is that?"

"The one that best describes your friend. Gail, I really meant to remain silent about Steve Tyner. I've known the truth about him for quite some time, and I've been tempted to tell you more often than you know. But I thought your disappointment wouldn't be worth whatever petty satisfaction I might get . . ."

"What *truth* are you talking about?"

"You see, your friend Steve came to see me, only a day or two after you met. He had a lot of questions to ask me, and he wouldn't get any answers from me until he told me the real nature of his interest."

"Oh," Gail said. "That. You mean the Bank. You mean because he works for the Fiduciary."

"Yes," Vanner said gravely. "I mean that. But I'm afraid I mean a great deal more. Because I know that Steve Tyner has deliberately underplayed the real significance of his work for the Bank."

"But he told me about what he was doing. He never hid anything from me!"

"I'm sure he didn't tell you *this*. That the Fiduciary has already decided to institute insanity proceedings against you. They're going to prepare a petition for indeterminate commitment, declaring you as mentally incompetent."

If he wanted her attention, he had it now.

"They needed evidence, of course, since forcible commitment is a serious business. That was Mr. Tyner's job, and I'm afraid it still is . . ."

"No—I won't believe that! I just won't!"

"He's described his assignment in full detail to me, Gail, and he's done more than that. He's attempted to enlist me as one of the two physicians required to pass judgment on your mental competence. He's made it very clear that my favorable response would be well rewarded by the Bank. I'm sure you know the name that describes that kind of offer."

She sank back against her pillows, making a deeper indentation as if her weight had suddenly increased.

"I wouldn't have told you this for the world," Vanner said softly, "until it occurred to me that your friend Steve might actually have some incredible parlay in mind. Not merely to see you committed, but to marry you as well, and find himself a very wealthy, very unencumbered young man . . ."

The light behind her eyes was gone.

"By the way," Vanner added, "the man at the Bank, the one you always mention, Saul Tedesco? Steve Tyner is his nephew. So you see, the scheme was a family affair."

Now the patient's expression was totally satisfactory to the attending physician.

Thirteen

"Let's see," Cecilia said, moistening a thumb and flipping through the loose-leaf pages, "How about Bhutan? Did you know they speak Dzonghka in Bhutan? Have you ever found a really *good* Dzonghak-English dictionary?"

"Try again," Steve told her, looking into a paper cup full of Scotch. It was the only receptacle Cecilia could find in the Pickering office. The liquor itself had been located in the bottom right-hand drawer of Perc McDougal's old desk, in a clay crock labeled GLUE. Luckily, Steve remembered the truth about its contents, or this after-hours meeting would have been dry as well as depressing.

"But listen, listen!" Cecilia said enthusiastically. "It must be a *fabulous* place, darling. Just listen to the words of the national anthem. *In the sandal-wood ornamented Kingdom of Dragonland . . .*"

"It's catchy," Steve said. "But I'd still prefer a country where they speak English."

"Well, here's one, right on the next page. Botswana. Official language, English. It's *diamond* country, darling. Just think what fun you'd have, strolling along the road and picking up huge fifty-carat diamonds. You could send me one as a present. Preferably in a ring, with baguettes."

"Sissy, something tells me you're not taking me seriously."

"It's you who don't take *me* seriously, darling." She lowered the Pickering directory and looked at him with solemnity darkening her Wedgwood-blue eyes. "I wish you'd tell me the truth about what happened."

"I told you the truth. I'm unemployed. I lost my job with the Bank, and my feet started to itch. So I came here to get them scratched. Now, will you please read on? Find a country I've *heard* of."

"Well, under B, there's Bolivia, Brazil, Bulgaria, and Burma, but there aren't any job openings there. According to this, they're fully staffed."

"I'm willing to go someplace that begins with C."

"How about Chad? We don't have anyone at all in Chad."

"Maybe Pickering doesn't *want* anyone in Chad. Maybe there isn't much news coming out of there."

"But there must be, darling, it's *huge*. As emerging nations go. Oh, dear, never mind. I just saw what the national anthem is. It starts out, *Chadians, up and to work*."

"You're right," Steve said. "I could do without that. Hey, whose idea was this 'national anthem' stuff?"

"Bill Cotler puts the book together these days, and he's mad about details like that. National anthems, national flower, national disease; you know. Ah, here's a *lovely* one, darling. I really think you should ask for an assignment in Equatorial Guinea. I'll go along, just so I can sing the anthem with you."

"All right, what is it?"

"Let's walk through the jungle of our immense happiness . . . Isn't that divine?"

"Super."

This time, Cecilia closed the book when she lowered it to the desk. "I'm not having any fun," she said. "I'm making all the jokes, and you're looking like the last scene of a Russian movie."

"Sorry, Sissy. It must be this glue I'm drinking."

"It's just so obvious that you have no immense happiness at all. And I *won't* believe that it's an employment problem. I'm sure it's that wench you told me about."

"Why do women always think romance motivates everything?"

"Loves makes the world go round, darling. And sometimes it makes men go around the world." She beamed with pleasure. "Isn't that clever? I'll have to remember that."

"Turn it into a national anthem."

"Did she find someone else?" Cecilia asked.

"Yes, if you must know. She found a psychiatrist."

"They *are* awfully sexy."

"Actually, he's a psychoanalyst too. And he did her the favor of analyzing me, the dirty son of a bitch."

"Heavens, darling, what language!"

"I told him about myself in strict confidence," Steve said bitterly. "There's supposed to be such a thing as privileged communication among psychiatrists, isn't there?"

"Between patient and doctor, yes."

"Don't split hairs. He knew that I was interested in helping the girl, not hurting her. He knew damned well that I wasn't out to prove there was anything *wrong* with her. Just the opposite."

"Of course I don't have the faintest idea what you're talking about."

"I still don't understand why he shafted me the way he did. He claimed that I was interfering with his therapy, but that wasn't reason enough. If the guy had one ounce of insight, he must have realized that I was crazy about her."

"Oh, dear." Cecilia sighed. "There goes my diamond."

"But he told her that I was in cahoots with the Bank. That I was working against her interests—which is putting it mildly."

"And what *are* her interests, darling? Needlepoint, chamber music, what?"

"You wouldn't understand," Steve said.

"Not from what you're telling me, that's flat."

"The worst part is," Steve said goomily, "that it's almost true. I *was* working against her, until I realized what a rotten job it was. But Vanner knew that I'd switched loyalties; he *had* to know it." He looked up from his paper cup. "Hey—maybe that's what happened. Maybe *he* switched loyalties, too!"

"Rave on, darling." Cecilia sighed.

"Now why didn't I think of that? There was no reason to shaft me if I was on *his* side. But what if he decided to be on *their* side? The Fiduciary Bank?"

"I've got a good one for you. When a man takes out too much money from his bank account, does he get withdrawal symptoms?"

"I asked him point-blank if he'd testify in Gail's behalf if they started proceedings against her. He didn't answer me. Maybe the Bank had already got to him. They could have realized that he's the best possible

witness they could have against her. Her own psychiatrist!"

"Your cup is leaking, darling."

But Steve was crushing and discarding it. "That
would be one very good reason for getting me out of
the picture, for turning Gail against me the way he
did! So that I wouldn't louse things up! Is that phone
alive?"

"Eek, I hope not."

He lifted it from the cradle, and heard a satisfying
dial tone. Then he called his uncle's home telephone
number and invited himself to Scarsdale for an over-
night visit.

Cecilia, disappointed, said: "Do you really have to
rush off?"

"I'm sorry. It's important."

"But I haven't even told you about those people yet.
The mountain accident people."

"You mean the Swanns?"

"Yes, darling, there was something on the teletype
about them this morning. They recovered the poor
man's body. Just the older one."

"What about his son?"

"No sign of him. Did you know he lived in Vienna?"

"Who did?"

"The younger one. I can't remember his name."

"Piers."

"Yes, lovely name. If I had a son, I'd like to call
him Piers. Of course, my chances of having a kid are
getting slimmer all the time. Although I wouldn't mind
having one out of wedlock—it's all the rage these
days."

"Sissy, what was that about Vienna?"

"Nothing, I just happened to notice that the teletype
gave Piers Swann's address as Vienna. He's lived there

for five years, even though his father's residence was in London. Now, about that wedlock business . . ."

"Goodnight, Sissy," Steve said. "Thanks for your help. And if you see Pickering tomorrow, tell him that I won't settle for anything less than Paris or Rome."

Tedesco and Steve's Aunt Sylvia were having dinner on the patio. Steve knew that his uncle detested eating outdoors ever since the day a fly got into his raisin pudding. But he adored his wife so much that he never quarreled with her desire to enjoy all the natural discomforts of their suburban home.

When Steve arrived, she immediately reacted by trotting into the kitchen to expand the dinner menu, despite his protest that he had already dined. Sylvia Tedesco enjoyed acting motherly toward Steve; but this evening, Saul Tedesco was anything but fatherly.

"Now what?" he grunted. "If you came here to say you changed your mind about the job, it's no dice. I've already told the directors that you've resigned."

"Sure you didn't say I was fired?"

"Maybe you should have been, considering your attitude."

"The Bank is lucky. They would have had to give me severance pay."

"The Bank doesn't have to do anything it doesn't want to do."

"A law unto itself, right?"

With the opening hostilities out of the way, they sat and regarded each other for a moment.

Then Steve said: "No, I can't believe you did what I think you did. I can't believe you'd be that sneaky. But maybe somebody else at the Fiduciary was."

"Go ahead, enjoy yourself."

"You know about Dr. Joel Vanner, of course. I told you I went to see him, and what he thought about

Gail Gunnerson's case. I'm sure the Bank didn't like what he said, since he thought she was perfectly sane."

Tedesco chewed the end off a cigar and spat it into the garden. "It's all right," he said. "Biodegradable."

"You knew what such an opinion could do to your notion of having Gail declared incompetent. If her own psychiatrist felt that she was fit to manage her estate, you'd have quite a battle on your hands when you went to court." Tedesco was fumbling in his pockets for a match, but couldn't find one. Steve, who still carried them even after quitting the habit, handed him a pack.

"Thanks," his uncle said.

"You couldn't let that situation stand, could you? And by *you* I don't mean you personally, Uncle, I mean someone at the Bank, someone over your head like Leonard Comfort, or Lowell Sankey or one of those guys. You knew the law would require you to produce medical testimony about Gail, so you hit on a perfect solution. Why not get Dr. Joel Vanner on *your* team? Then there wouldn't be the slightest doubt about success."

"Finished?"

"Not yet. I saw Gail yesterday, and she informed me that Vanner knew all about me, about what I was hired to do, about who was behind me, and even the fact that we're related. In case you're interested, I had asked Gail Gunnerson to marry me."

"Well! Now that's a piece of news."

"She didn't give me her answer until yesterday. Guess what it was?"

"No?"

"She told me her reason for turning me down. She said she wasn't sure she'd be happy with a husband who was trying to lock her up in a madhouse. Women are funny, aren't they? No wonder Freud couldn't understand them."

"Finished now?"

"Yes," Steve said.

"Good." Tedesco took the cigar out of his mouth and punctuated his speech with it. "Point one, you're wrong. Point two, you're a damned fool. Point three, you have a terrible memory. I'll start with point three."

"I'm listening."

"That report you gave us on your visit to the psychiatrist. You didn't say flat-out that he diagnosed Miss Gunnerson as A number one normal. In fact, you said that he was trying to find out what kind of traumatic experience she had in her childhood that drove her off the edge. Something about a door, am I right?"

Steve swallowed. "Okay, there was something, but it *was* in her childhood."

"You admitted that the trauma or whatever it's called was still present, that it was stuck in her brain like one of those old unexploded bombs from World War II they used to find in the cellars in London."

"I don't remember making any such analogy."

"Okay, maybe I made it up myself. But I didn't make up the fact that she was having more hallucinations, that she was getting worse all the time. Now for point two."

"About being a damned fool?"

"That goes without saying. The world is full of girls with dynamite looks; what do you need with a mental case?" He stopped Steve's reply with an upraised hand. "Never mind. We'll go straight to point one."

"You're going to tell me I'm wrong."

"You were never wronger about anything, Nephew. Nobody has been sneaking around to get Gail Gunnerson committed; nobody *has* to do that. If she keeps on the way she's going, she'll probably commit herself voluntarily—"

"That's not so."

"I think the girl is smarter than you are, Steven, smarter than any of us, maybe, and the intelligent part of her brain is watching over the part that's disintegrating, and recognizing that something has to be done."

"You don't know her the way I do. She's rather kill herself than go into a mental hospital."

"With that girl's money, she could buy her *own* hospital and be the only patient. Anyway, there hasn't been any coercion or collusion of any kind, not by me, not by Leonard Comfort or Lowell Sankey or anyone else at the Bank. I'm telling you this on your mother's grave, Steven, if you'll pardon the old-fashioned expression. Dr. Vanner hasn't sold his soul to us, because we never made him an offer for it. Is that good enough for you?"

Steve slumped in the wicker chair. Sylvia Tedesco emerged with a mountainous load of chicken breasts and legs, smiling all over her plump face. "I told you there was plenty, didn't I?"

Later, chewing dutifully, Steve asked: "You honestly never even talked to Vanner, Uncle?"

"It occurred to me," he said. "I looked him up in the medical directory, just to see what kind of credentials he had, in case he ever *did* testify."

"How were they?"

Tedesco shrugged. "He didn't seem to be very strong opposition. He wasn't even listed."

"What directory was it?"

"Some book the head shrinkers put out. Listing their degrees, their fancy titles. Your friend Vanner wasn't there."

The unlisted Dr. Vanner said: "Gail, I think it's time I told you about yourself."

Her head barely moved on the pillow. But the pupils of her eyes shifted toward him, exposing blood-shot corners.

"I'm going to tell you what I think really happened that night, the night they came for your mother. I don't mean that I can reconstruct the events, or tell you exactly what shape your fantasy took when . . . that door opened."

Now her eyes slid to the door. She said: "Could I have some water?"

Vanner poured her a glass. "But even if I can't define the *thing* for you, and maybe erase it from your subconscious forever, I think I can tell you *why* it all happened. And maybe, just maybe, your comprehension of the process will help you *see* the creature of your imagination again. See it, recognize it, lose your fear of it—the fear that's still torturing you. Do you understand what I'm saying?"

Her head moved slightly; Vanner accepted it as a nod.

"What happened that night didn't *start* that night, Gail. That's the first thing you have to realize. It was the culmination of a neurotic disorder. Yes, I know that six seems like a very young age for a neurosis, but I'm afraid it was already in the budding. Because childhood has a built-in complex. It's called the Oedipus complex—I'm sure you've heard of it."

"What time is it?" Gail said.

He tried not to show his annoyance. "Never mind the hour," he said. "It's late. You probably want to sleep. But I think you'll sleep better if you hear me out. Gail, all children face this conflict, and the way they turn out depends on whether or not they find a healthy solution to it. You didn't. Do you grasp what

I'm saying? You did not. It wasn't your fault. It was the circumstances, of both your mother's ill health and your father's absence. You loved your parents, Gail, but like all little girls, you loved your mother best. It's a very demanding thing, that kind of love. Sometimes, it disappoints. Disappoints very badly. And the greater the disappointment, the more the child turns against the mother. She loses what we call the cathexis for her. In your case, your cathexis was seriously weakened by your mother's health. Because the sicker she got, the more she ignored you. Isn't that right?"

Now Gail's nod was perceptible. "Yes," she said. "It's true. She didn't know I was alive then."

"That was when you turned to your father for the love you needed. You began to prefer him to her. It became so strong a preference that you actually resented your mother for standing between you. You were jealous of her, Gail; at the tender age of six, you were the rival for your father's love. And a child tends to think in simple, direct terms; understands only simple, direct solutions to problems. For you, the simplest solution to the triangle would have been your mother's death."

If she had been less sedated, Gail might have voiced her shock or resentment. Now a look had to suffice.

"I know it sounds drastic. And in most cases, maturity ameliorates the conflict without any trouble. But you weren't given a chance to work it out. Because while the conflict was still raging, two events occurred in your life. The father whom you loved was taken away from you. He went to war and was killed; but the concept of "war" was beyond you. What you actually felt was that your mother drove your father away, removed him from your life so that you could no longer win him away from her. You resented her all the more for that. And when the word came that he had been killed, your sense of loss was complicated by a sense of betrayal. No, I don't expect you to recall those feelings now. But they were there."

"And then, something even more terrible occurred. Your mother died, too. The fact that she died by her own hand was concealed from you. Perhaps that was a mistake. Perhaps it might have helped you to know that her decision to leave the world was her own, that it had nothing to do with you. Do you see what I'm driving at, Gail?"

"No."

"You felt an enormous guilt at your mother's death, because it was exactly what you were wishing for."

"No! I couldn't have been!"

"To this day you don't want to recall your true feelings because they seem just as terrible now as they did then. When your mother died, you felt responsible. And you knew that guilt was followed by punishment."

"Punishment . . ."

"Yes. And your unconscious didn't wait long to deliver that punishment. It came that very night, Gail. It came through . . . that door."

She looked at it again, still without expression. "I don't remember," she said.

"You'll have to, Gail. For your own sake, you'll have to remember it again, see it again, face it down once and for all!"

"I think I'd die if I did," Gail said.

Dr. Vanner said nothing—to her.

Mrs. Bellinger misinterpreted his tired gait and down-turned mouth and asked if Gail was any worse. He said no; he said he had given her something to help her sleep, that she would be better in the morning. Mrs. Bellinger hinted that she could use "something" herself; she was sleeping so poorly these nights. Vanner frowned and said that he wasn't able to accommodate her. The housekeeper apologized for the request; she offered him a cup of tea in expiation. Vanner suggested it might be too late in the evening, but since Mrs. Bellinger wasn't retiring yet, he accepted graciously. Mrs. Bellinger decided that he was quite a respectable sort of physician after all, even if he didn't carry a small black bag. She offered to serve the tea in the parlor, but he said the kitchen would do fine. Now Mrs. Bellinger thought he had charm as well as professionalism. She produced some small cookies to go with the beverage.

"Aren't you joining me?" Dr. Vanner said. When she merely blushed in response, he said: "I really wish you would. I'd like to talk to you about something."

The housekeeper sat, deferentially and somewhat precariously, on the edge of a chair.

"I've been speaking to Miss Gunnerson," he said, "about the night her mother passed away. The night that she took ill. I'm sure that's a night you've never forgotten."

"And never will," she said. "Not if I'm a hundred."

"I'm sure you were very devoted to Mrs. Gunnerson."

Mrs. Bellinger lifted a shoulder. "She was a sweet sad woman, but I can't say I ever really knew her. By the time I was hired, she was already acting . . . the way she did. So quiet and shy and keeping to herself, not talking to anyone but her husband, hardly even to her own child. Oh, it was bad enough when she passed away, but that wasn't the worst of the night for me. It was seeing that little girl go all to pieces that way."

"Yes," Vanner said. "I'm sure that wasn't very pleasant."

"She was only six years old, you know. So sad to lose both her parents in the same year, and no family left except *those* two." She produced a mighty sniff of disapproval.

"Those two? You mean her uncle and her cousin? The Swanns?"

"Yes—the Swanns. Now *there* were a pair of birds for you. Her uncle with his high-and-mighty way, never stepping foot into this house until someone died in it, never writing his own brother unless it was to borrow money. He was the poor one of the family, you see, but he acted like the King of England. Which is where they lived, those two. Him and that awful boy."

"His son, you mean." Vanner stretched out his legs under the kitchen table, beginning to relax and enjoy himself.

"I never did care for little boys. We were lucky in our family, we had nothing but girls. But except for Emily, all my sisters are dead now. His name was Piers. Funny name for a boy, isn't it? And he was full of the devil, with his aunt lying dead upstairs, the disrespect was something awful."

Now Vanner concealed a smile behind an uplifted teacup. "Were they here very long? Miss Gunnerson's relatives?"

"Not more than a day. Just long enough to bury the poor woman, and then they went back home to London."

"Then there weren't many people in this house that night."

"No, it was a terribly empty and lonely place, I can tell you. All day long there had been people in, coming to pay their last respects. But everyone was gone that night, even the two servants, the upstairs and the downstairs girl, Jennie and Missy their names were. They were carrying on so much with their crying, Mr. Swann sent them both home. And of course they were never needed again, considering what happened, Gail getting sick the way she did and the house being shut up for almost six years before she came out of That Place . . ."

"Tell me about the boy," Vanner said. "He seems to have made quite an impression on you."

"I would have liked to have made an impression on *him*, if you know what I mean. On his rear end. Running all over the house, sliding down the bannister like it was some kind of amusement park."

"Little boys don't understand death, do they? Or little girls, for that matter."

"No," Mrs. Bellinger said mournfully. "I suppose I can't really blame children for the way they are. The grownups make such a fuss about it. I mean, death itself isn't so bad, not if you believe in the Eternal Reward, but I hate the trappings that go with it, the embalming and so forth." She shivered.

Vanner yawned, beginning to lose interest. But now Mrs. Bellinger decided to pour herself a cup of tea.

"I'll never forget that man Shanks," she said. "He looked like the Angel of Death himself. I swear, that uncle of Gail's must have gone out of his way to find such an ugly man to do that ugly work."

"Who?" Vanner said.

"Shanks, the undertaker. He came that night to take poor Mrs. Gunnerson away. He was bad enough to look at the first time, but when he came again, and the hour being close to midnight, and me alone in the house—well! Let me tell you, that was enough to give me goose flesh for days, just the sight of that man's ugly face in the doorway."

"Close to midnight? That was a strange time to call for a body."

"No, he came first about seven, I think, or maybe even six-thirty. He came back that night because he had forgotten something—his briefcase. Said he'd left it in the parlor. I was heating up some milk for Gail, I didn't want it to boil over, so I told him to find it and let himself out. Strange how you remember a little thing like that for years and years. Would you like some more tea?"

"No," Vanner said, covering his empty cup with his palm. He was feeling weary again. He stood up and stretched cramped back muscles. It had been too long a day. "I really have to be going now, Mrs. Bellinger. Sorry about the sleeping pill."

"That's all right, I never should have asked. And do you know something else? That man Shanks didn't even find his briefcase. I found it, the next morning, in Mrs. Gunnerson's room. When I went to make up the poor woman's deathbed."

"So he left without it?"

"Yes, he came all that way for nothing. And it was just a couple of minutes after I heard him leave that the child started to scream. That awful screaming."

Vanner paused to watch her bring the steaming brew to her lips. He looked at his own empty cup, at the tea leaves, staring at the pattern like a gypsy looking for portents. "Heard him leave?" he asked.

"Yes. Heard the front door slam. I remember thinking that he had a nerve, slamming that door so loud."

"Then you didn't *see* him go out the door?"

"No, I was in here. In the kitchen."

Vanner returned to the table and sat down. His weariness was gone. "Mrs. Bellinger," he said. "Isn't it possible that Mr. Shanks didn't give up looking for his briefcase? When he failed to find it in the parlor?"

"I don't know what you mean."

"Isn't it possible that he *remembered* leaving his briefcase on the upper floor, when he called for Mrs. Gunnerson's body? He could have gone upstairs to find it. Doesn't that seem logical to you, Mrs. Bellinger?"

"But if he'd gone to Mrs. Gunnerson's room, he *would* have found it. It was on a chair, just inside the door."

"The door," Vanner said softly.

"What?"

"I was thinking about bedroom doors, Mrs. Bellinger, and how much they look alike."

The cup clattered. "Oh, Holy Mary, Mother of God, you don't suppose——"

"Mr. Shanks didn't know this house, did he? He might easily have forgotten which door led into which room. Couldn't he, Mrs. Bellinger?" He put his hand on her plump arm; it had grown bumpy and cold. "You know something?" he said. "All this time I've been analyzing the wrong person. I should have talked to you long ago."

He was smiling.

Fourteen

"May I have the name, please?"

"Dr. Joel Vanner."

"Were you the attending physician?"

"Pardon?"

"Is that your name, or the name of the deceased?"

Vanner chuckled, but smothered the sound as inappropriate. He was sure that chuckles weren't considered good form, even in the outer offices of the Strathmore Funeral Home. The face of the young man behind the Directoire desk was also inappropriate to the surroundings; tie a blue bandanna around his neck and he would have looked like a country western singer instead of a mortician.

"I'm not here to make . . . arrangements," Vanner said. "I came to inquire about someone who was employed here, who may still be employed perhaps. A Mr. Shanks. I don't know his first name."

"Shanks? Nobody by that name working here."

"I believe he may have owned the Strathmore at one time, or managed it, at least."

"How long ago?"

"I'm afraid my information is almost twenty years old," Vanner admitted. "But I'm quire sure it's accurate. Strathmore did the 'arrangements' for a woman named Cressie Gunnerson, and your Mr. Shanks was in charge."

The man tugged at a straw-blond forelock. "I've only been here six months, so I really wouldn't know about the management then."

"I thought you might be able to help me locate him, in some other establishment perhaps. It's really quite important that I get in touch with him."

"No, I don't think I can help you. I don't know many people in the business; I've only been in it a year myself."

"Enjoying it?" Vanner said. A grin split his facial hair. The fledgling mortician's red face reddened further, and he stood up.

"I'll go ask Mr. Feeny," he said. "He's the general manager; he's been here since the Strathmore opened. Maybe he can remember."

"I'd appreciate it," Vanner said. "You're very kind."

What he also appreciated was a moment alone in the padded stillness of the room. He hadn't had much time to chew over, savor, and digest the new information that had come his way so fortuitously the night before. When he arrived home he had been immediately assaulted by a tempestuous Cassandra, insanely love-starved after days of neglect. Vanner cursed the beast when he saw that she had expressed her resentment in no uncertain terms all over the "analyst" couch which represented his only capital investment in the furnished professional apartment he had engaged. If his mood hadn't been so benign, he might have fulfilled his daily promise to put her to sleep. That had been Cassandra's threatened fate when he first adopted her; the building's landlady had tired of submitting to the big dog's clumsy love-hunger and outraged excesses, and was considering a one-way trip to the pound. Vanner had intervened, not because he liked dogs, but because he felt that Cassandra's presence in his life would create an air of permanence, would make him appear to be a settled citizen instead of a recent immigrant. Cassandra had done her job; now her usefulness was over. Vanner put her leash around her neck, and took the dog to Central Park, braving the dangerous darkness. As he approached the Sheep Meadow he let Cassandra slip her collar. She was accustomed to romping unfettered in the daytime; in the darkness, she seemed hesitant. "Go on, Cass, go on, girl," he urged, slapping her rump. The dog was emboldened and went bounding after a scrap of paper teased along by the wind, probably thinking it was a rabbit. Vanner left the park quickly, discarding the leash in a wire trash basket. Then he went home and slept unbrokenly until morning.

There had been no time until now to muse over the wonderful simplicity of the answer Mrs. Bellinger had so helpfully provided. Simplicity! That was why it had escaped all those complex thinkers at the Mead Clinic. They had been too busy searching for anti-cathexes, for endopsychic conflicts, for the convoluted mechanism of Gail Gunnerson's moral anxieties. They had been too concerned with analyzing a dream which had never occurred. No, Gail hadn't dreamed herself a nightmare: the nightmare was flesh and blood and bone, between six and seven feet of it, terrifying in his ugliness and ugly in his terrifying purpose. *He's come to your mother,* Piers had told her. *He's going to take her away. He's going to put her in a wooden box.* Vanner shook his head admiringly at the direct-ness of children. *That's what an undertaker does,* Piers had told the six-year-old Gail. *He puts you in a box and then buries you under the ground . . .*

But that wasn't all *this* undertaker had done. This undertaker may have known where the bodies were buried, but he was forgetful in other things. Poor Mr. Shanks had lost his briefcase. Vanner pictured some shaggy pouchy leather thing containing a neat note-book filled with notations about funeral dates and floral arrangements, Shanks' personal Book of the Dead. He had forgotten his precious briefcase, and he had returned to the Gunnerson house to find it, and had encountered a crusty, footsore housekeeper un-willing to sympathize with his loss. He had been un-able to locate his beloved property in the parlor, so he had decided to ascend the stairs to the second floor, to search the most likely room, the sanctum of the dead woman herself. But it wasn't Cressie Gunnerson's door he had opened. It was her little girl's.

And Gail had awakened.

Sleep-filled, tear-irritated eyes opening, blinking, seeing.

The whole crooked black length of him, silhouetted in the doorway.

A step into the room, and her night light shed just enough illumination to let her view his grotesque, un-forgetting features.

The undertaker was back.

The man who put people in wooden boxes had re-turned.

And this time, he had come for her.

"Good news."

Vanner's head snapped around so suddenly he could feel the vertebrae crack. The country western singer was smiling at him. "Mr. Feeny not only knew Mr. Shanks, he used to work for him. His full name was Calvin Shanks, and you were right: he once owned the Strathmore. He sold it to Mr. Feeny and two other people when he retired."

"Retired," Vanner echoed flatly.

"Confidentially," the mortician said, "I gather it was an enforced retirement. Mr. Feeny says that Mr.

Shanks had a drinking problem and wasn't in the best of health."

Even more dejected: "How long ago was this?"

"About five years."

"Did Shanks leave the city?"

"No, I'm quite sure he's still here. Mr. Feeny said that he gets a Christmas card from him every year, and they're always postmarked Brooklyn. I can't give you the address, but maybe he's in the directory."

"That was one place I didn't think to try," Vanner said wryly. "The Brooklyn phone book."

He did, within the next half hour. Calvin L. Shanks was listed at 8891 Utica. When Vanner dialed the number and heard the vocalized evidence of Mr. Shanks' continued existence, he marveled again at Destiny's kind, continuing, almost loving cooperation.

Calvin Shanks occupied the lower floor of a two-family house that resembled in every detail some two dozen other brick two-family houses on the block. There were other similarities in the neighborhood, a homogeneity of automobiles, children, shrubbery, wives. Most of the neighborhood's male population had left on business, but Calvin Shanks had no other enterprise to attend to besides the scraggly garden behind the house and the housekeeping of his own cramped quarters. But Shanks bore little resemblance to his neighbors. He was unique. If anything, Vanner thought ungrammatically, twenty years' passage had made him *more* unique.

Until he saw him again, Vanner could only recall that Shanks was a black-clad, insectlike figure, a praying mantis in mourning clothes. Now he recollected the face of the man as well, a face pre-caricatured by nature, the eyes like licorice balls rolling in pouches of skin, the prominent nose, the downturned mouth and trowel chin. Time and alcoholic abuse hadn't altered the face, even if it had stopped the body.

He was the undertaker. Still.

"Vanner," he said loudly, realizing that Shanks had suffered some hearing loss. "*Dr.* Vanner."

"Didn't understand what you wanted on the phone," Shanks said. "What was it you wanted me for?"

"I told you that it concerned a patient of mine, a Miss Gail Gunnerson. I'm sure the name doesn't mean anything to you, but you may remember that you buried her mother, in March of 1955. When you were in charge of the Strathmore Funeral Home."

"No," Shanks said, shaking his head. "I don't know the name. You can't expect me to remember all the names. too many of them."

"I think I can help you remember this one. The Gunnerson house is on Schuyler Avenue, in Manhattan. It's a town house, a mansion, really. The Gunnersons were very wealthy. Mr. Theodore Gunnerson was very wealthy, but he was killed in Korea. He married an actress named Cressie Blake. That's the one who died. Is any of that familiar to you?"

Shanks' head was moving from side to side, resisting the effort to remember.

"My patient was only six years old at the time, Mr. Shanks, a little girl who was orphaned by her mother's death. She was very badly shaken up by the whole thing, of course, but something else happened that night that shook her up even more. Something *you* may have been responsible for."

Now the head was still, the licorice eyes rolling around to look at Vanner curiously.

"What are you talking about?"

"I'm a psychiatrist, you see. I'm trying to help this young lady overcome a severe psychiatric problem, one that endangers her health and perhaps even her life. That night, she suffered what we call a 'trauma,' and it sent her into a mental hospital at that very young age. Only recently I learned the *cause* of that trauma, Mr. Shanks, and it seems to have been *you*."

Vanner let the last word hang between them like a taut string.

"*Me?*" Shanks gasped. "What the hell are you blaming me for? I didn't give nobody any traumas, I don't even know what they are!"

"You called for the body of Cressie Gunnerson on the evening of March the twelfth, 1955. You brought two men with you from the mortuary, most likely Mr. Feeny was one of them. You took the body away. But about four hours later, you went *back* to the Gunnerson house. It was somewhere between eleven and midnight. You went back because you had forgotten something there. Do you remember what it was?"

Shanks' hand went searching for his mouth. The slit was so thin, it was a wonder he found it.

"Forgot something . . . Yes . . . I guess I remember about that. About losing my fountain pen or something in somebody's house . . ."

"Briefcase," Vanner said.

"Yes, briefcase. That was it. Only I don't remember whose house it was. Or the name of the party."

"Gunnerson," Vanner said, helpful as always. "Try to remember the name, Mr. Shanks, because you can be sure that the police remember it."

"*Police?* What have the *pólice* got to do with this?"

"I know it happened a very long time ago. But that doesn't really matter. Even when crimes haven't been solved for years and years, that doesn't mean the criminal can escape punishment."

"Who's a *criminal?* What are you using words like *criminal* for?"

"No matter how many years pass," Vanner said,

"there are certain offenses that never get forgotten —or forgiven, for that matter. Especially when they involve helpless little children. You know, policemen have families, too, small kids of their own. They're hypersensitive about such things."

"*What* things?" Shanks said, and Vanner was gratified to see that he was pleading for information now.

"You came back to that house, Mr. Shanks, because you wanted your briefcase. You spoke to the housekeeper, a woman named Bellinger, who told you to look for it yourself. But you couldn't find it in the parlor, so you decided to go upstairs, to the bedroom. You didn't ask the housekeeper's permission—you were afraid she would refuse. So you went upstairs all by yourself. Tell me if that's true or false?"

Shanks pulled his hand from his mouth and exposed thin lips as arid as a desert. He shuffled toward a cupboard and took out a bottle, pouring himself a shot glass of liquor without offering Vanner a drink or an excuse.

"What about it, Mr. Shanks?"

"Yes, that's right," he said. "I went upstairs. All I wanted was my briefcase. I needed it. I kept all my notes and things in it, all my working stuff." He downed the contents of the glass soundlessly.

"And did you find the briefcase?"

"Yes, I found it. Course I did. In the dead lady's room, where I left it."

"No," Vanner said somberly. "You didn't find your briefcase in Mrs. Gunnerson's room. The housekeeper had it sent over to the Strathmore the next day. You didn't find it because you didn't open *the right door.*"

"That ain't so!"

"It was the first time you were in that house; it wasn't your fault that you mistook one door for another. You didn't realize you were making a mistake when you opened the door of Gail Gunnerson's room. It wasn't you fault, Mr. Shanks, was it?"

"No!" Shanks said. "It wasn't my fault! I didn't know it was the kid's room, I didn't even know there *was* a kid!"

"Just a simple error—isn't that right? You just opened the door and walked in and thought you were in the right place."

"That was it!"

"Only what was *wrong* was that the child screamed. She saw you coming in, this little six-year-old girl, and she was scared out of her wits."

"She scared *me,* let me tell you! I went down those stairs like a bat out of hell! I got out of that house as fast as I could travel!"

"But why? Why didn't you stay to explain?"

"I just told you! I got scared!! I wasn't supposed to have been *upstairs.* I told the woman I was going to look in the parlor. Who knows what she would have thought? I mean, people can misunderstand these things!"

"Yes," Vanner said. "Or maybe they understand them only too well. Maybe they know there are men who have strange notions about little girls."

"What?"

"I'm a psychiatrist, Mr. Shanks, I told you that. And I know very well that there are men with—aberrations, men who don't really care for grown women, only for sweet little girls of five or six or seven, charming little innocents with pretty faces and smooth little arms and legs . . ."

The crooked frame of Calvin Shanks seemed to be telescoping in some surrealistic fashion. He folded himself into an awkward seating position, and luckily found a day bed beneath him. He looked up at Vanner with a fear that was almost worshipful.

"No," he said. "I never did anything wrong to that little girl. I didn't even know she was there. Don't tell people things like that, mister, they'll think it was like —those other times. And it wasn't. I swear it wasn't!"

"Those *other* times?"

"Those other things they say I did. Only those weren't such little girls, they weren't that young, I swear!"

Vanner wanted to laugh, the sweet laughter of fulfillment and triumph. Destiny wasn't merely cooperating now; Destiny was his equal partner.

"Please don't worry, Mr. Shanks," he said, in the soothing tones of a physician. "Everything is going to be all right. For you and for my patient. As long as you help me *make* things right."

"But how? I won't have to go to the police?"

"No," Vanner said. "Of course not. This is the place where I want you to go. This evening."

He removed a scrap of paper from his pocket. He had already written out Gail Gunnerson's address in large, clear letters.

Fifteen

"Steve Tyner called," Gail told her doctor.

Vanner, taking her pulse, felt his own accelerate. But he remained unruffled outwardly, and merely voiced an uninterested "Oh?"

"He called three times, as a matter of fact. I didn't

speak to him, of course; Mrs. Bellinger did. That woman becomes more impossible every day. I told her clearly that I didn't want to talk to him, but every time he phoned she'd buzz me and ask the same question."

"Mrs. Bellinger sounds a bit partisan."

"She is, I'm afraid. But she doesn't know what Steve Tyner really is. She thinks he's just some nice young man I had a little spat with, and that we're sure to kiss and make up. What are the elves doing in my aorta?"

"Your heart is fine." Vanner smiled, placing her arm underneath the coverlet. "In more ways than one. I don't doubt for one minute that you'll find someone a great deal more deserving than Mr. Tyner."

"He spoke to Mrs. Bellinger," Gail said wistfully. "She reported his conversation, even though I insisted that I wasn't interested." She stroked the tip of the stuffed bear's worn-down nose. "Steve is going away. He's taking a job with that news bureau and going off to somewhere exotic like Timbuktu. Is there still a Timbuktu?"

"I suppose so. And I don't envy the Timbuktuans."

"I wish I didn't," Gail said, and turned her head into the pillow. Vanner waited to ascertain if there would be sniffles of remorse. When there were none, he picked up the plastic cylinder from the table and dropped four of the tiny white pills onto his palm. He regarded them speculatively for a moment, and then returned one of them to the bottle.

"Here," he said. "Time for your medicine."

"Do I have to?"

"Yes, little girl," Vanner answered, in parental mockery. "I know you hate to feel drowsy all the time, but that's only a side effect. The benefits outweigh the disadvantages."

"They make me feel totally weightless. I'm sure it's

the way the astronauts must feel. Just floating in space, never touching solid ground. Only it's even more than that. I feel as if I'm floating in time, too. This morning I looked at the clock and I wasn't sure if it was six-thirty in the morning or the evening. How much longer do I have to keep this up?"

"Until your doctor tells you that you've had enough bed rest. Or until Mission Control tells you that you're ready for Earth gravity again."

"Gravity," Gail said. "What a strange word that is. 'The gravity of the situation.' Does it have anything to do with that?"

"I'm a psychiatrist, not a philologist."

"And grave. I'm sure it has something to do with the grave." Now she turned to look at him. "Aren't you going to tell me that's morbid?"

"Not if you've already told yourself," Vanner said, and poured her a glass of water.

Gail took the pills, not commenting on the odd number until after she had swallowed them. Then she said: "Three pills. You really want me out of it tonight, don't you?"

Vanner answered delicately. "I want you to sleep better than you did last night."

"But they don't help me sleep. They just make the room go around. My bedroom goes into orbit every night; have I reported that symptom?"

"We're very big on the space analogies this evening, aren't we?" Vanner smiled. "Well, just tuck yourself into the capsule and forget about the 'gravity of the situation.' It isn't nearly as bad as you think. You had a good night, even if you didn't sleep well. No hallucinations, no more ghosts or hobgoblins appearing at the door . . . I'd say that was a good sign."

"Would you?"

"So just stay in bed, Gail. Don't decide to talk any

space walks like you did last night. Oh, yes, Mrs. Bellinger ratted on you—I know all about it."

"I just went to the kitchen," Gail said. "I was suddenly very hungry, so I went downstairs to heat up some of that stew. I couldn't eat a thing yesterday, not after you told me about . . . Steve."

"Well, I'm glad you regained your appetite anyway, even in the middle of the night."

"No," Gail said flatly. "The moment I saw Mrs. Bellinger's stew in that big iron pot in the refrigerator, I lost my appetite again. I just sat down at the kitchen table and cried all over the Formica . . ." She bit her lip, and forcibly changed the subject. "Listen, speaking about walking—how's Cassandra?"

Vanner snapped the cap back on the bottle. "Well . . ." he said.

"What on earth does that poor dog do when you're away? I've thought about that several times. Does she sleep on the couch in your office?"

"To tell you the honest truth," Vanner said gently, "the news isn't good about Cass."

"What do you mean?"

"I didn't want to mention this before, but Cass hasn't been well lately. Her behavior left a great deal to be desired. So did her self-control, if you know what I mean."

"No, I don't."

"Cassandra became terribly accident prone. And full of all sorts of whims and fancies."

"What caused it all?"

Vanner shrugged. "I don't know. Some infection, probably. That's what the vet said. It affected her mind. She began to bark and snarl at people she was ordinarily fond of. Howl in the middle of the night as if the devil had her by the tail. She wasn't getting any better—just worse. Finally, I did the only possible thing."

"What was that?"

"She had to be put to sleep. That's always a difficult decision, of course, but it had to be done."

"Oh, how awful."

"The poor beast was suffering," Vanner said, touching her shoulder. "She was no good to herself or to anyone else. She went peacefully to sleep, Gail, a sleep without nightmares . . . Sometimes, that's the only answer. You know that, don't you?"

"Yes," Gail Gunnerson whispered.

He sought out Mrs. Bellinger in the kitchen and caught her in the act of applying a pink rhomboid to the bottom of her foot. She put her shoe on quickly and asked if he would like some tea or coffee. Vanner said: "As a matter of fact, I came to ask if *you'd* like something."

"Me?"

"I was sorry that I couldn't give you anything to help you sleep last night. I realized that it's just as important to Gail for *you* to be well-rested."

"Didn't close my eyes until three in the morning," the housekeeper sighed. "What it is, Doctor, I keep *listening* all the time, I keeping thinking I hear that poor girl's voice calling out for me."

"I understand your anxiety. That's why I brought some pills with me tonight. I'm sure they'll help." He reached into his pocket, but the wall phone demanded answering. Mrs. Bellinger picked it up and said hello, listened, and then shook her head sadly. "No, I don't think so, Mr. Tyner. You know what she said those other times. Also, the doctor's here now, and I think he'd rather she get some sleep . . . Yes, Dr. Vanner . . . Well, I really wouldn't know." She looked quizzically at her company and asked: "Mr. Tyner wants to know if he can talk to you."

Vanner thought a moment. "Yes, certainly." He took the phone from her. "Tyner!" he said cheerfully, as if to an old friend.

"I've been trying to reach Gail all day," Steve said. "Thanks to you, she won't even talk to me."

"Gail tells me that you're leaving town. For Timbuktu, she said. She admitted she might have gotten that detail wrong."

"She has. I've been offered a spot in the Rome bureau of the Pickering agency."

"Rome! Wonderful! Say hello to Marco for me. He's a waiter at Hostaria dell' Orso. Mention my name and he'll be good to you."

"I want to know how Gail is."

"Sorry. I don't think I care to discuss my patient with someone not related to her." He suppressed a smile when he heard Steve's scatological reply. Then he said: "All right, if you really want to know, her condition is serious. She's on an emotional critical list, and the next few days or even hours may determine whether or not she needs to be hospitalized. That was one of the reasons why I suggested that you don't try to reach her now. In case you didn't realize it, Mr. Tyner, you're one of the primary causes of this crisis."

"How about yourself?" Steve said hotly. "If you hadn't told her about my job with the Fiduciary—"

"Yes," Vanner said, his voice the opposite temperature. "If I hadn't told her the truth and allowed her to go on believing that your relationship was genuine—"

"Speaking of *genuine*," Steve said, "how come you're not listed by the American Psychiatric Association, Doc?"

The telephone dial seemed to be spinning in front

of Vanner's eyes. He overcame the momentary dizziness by spreading his fingertips against the kitchen wall.

"I beg your pardon," he said. "What was that remark?"

"I said," Steve answered, "that you're not listed in a single medical directory. I called the Association and they said that your listing might be too recent to make the latest edition of their head shrinkers manual, but they had no record of your application for listing."

"Who said I was required to apply?"

"I also called the New York State Board of Regents, the people who license you guys, and they couldn't find any record of any Joel Vanner, either. Where'd you get your diploma, Doc, in a box of Crackerjacks?"

"I don't intend to give you a rundown of my credentials, Mr. Tyner. But since you raised the point—if you had examined my diploma you would have realized that it wasn't issued to me in this country, which is why it's taking the Board so long to get me on their roster."

"Well, where was it issued—Timbuktu?"

"Vienna," Vanner said. "The University of Vienna. Now, if you don't mind, I have to see my patient."

He hung up without waiting for a reaction and turned to his "patient," Mrs. Bellinger, who sat with crossed fingers at the kitchen table. Vanner smiled at her and reached into his pocket for the small envelope containing the sleeping capsules.

"Take both of them now," he advised. "They'll take about half an hour to start working, but by the time you're ready for bed I'm sure you'll sleep very soundly."

"Thank you, Doctor," she said.

Vanner watched her swallow them. Each capsule contained enough milligrams of phenobarbital to narcotize a young bull for the rest of the night. Two of them should be a guarantee of noninterference. Already convinced of their potency, Mrs. Bellinger began to yawn within seconds of ingesting them, and Vanner chuckled.

"Maybe you should get to bed right now, Mrs. Bellinger."

"Are you sure Gail won't need me any more?"

"I'm sure Gail will be asleep herself very soon. And don't worry about me. I'll let myself out."

Mrs. Bellinger's parting look was one of gratitude and trust. Sweet old thing, Vanner thought. His mood was mellow. He even felt kindly toward Steve Tyner, despite Tyner's crude attempt at reprisal. Vanner wasn't concerned about the credentials problem, since Dr. Joel Vanner was already being phased out of existence. That afternoon, upon returning from Brooklyn, he had packed up the few possessions that were his own in the furnished professional apartment, including the diploma, and left the landlady a final rent check and a brief note concerning his sudden departure to attend a psychiatric conference "abroad." His bags were in the trunk of his rented car; his airline ticket was in the glove compartment—that knowledge gave Vanner a delicious feeling of liberation.

He went into the Gunnerson parlor and poured himself a glass of sherry, the only potable available. He didn't drink ordinarily, but there was something about this evening which demanded the ceremony of lifting glass to lips. It wasn't for the need of courage, he told himself. He had already convinced himself of his own fortitude; he was fully aware of possessing remarkable determination. He toasted himself in frank admiration of his qualities. Then he sat back and waited for the doorbell to ring.

Shanks arrived a few minutes after the appointed hour of ten. Vanner wasn't surprised; he was sure that the ex-undertaker had made a troubled circuit of the block before summoning the nerve to reenter the Gunnerson town house. He must have looked at that structure in dreadful remembrance of the night of March 12, 1955; he must have dreaded even more the assignment that had brought him back here after nearly twenty years. Vanner had assured him that his mission was only therapeutic, but the moment he saw Shanks' stooping figure and trembling hands, the thin lips smacking moisture out of his near-toothless mouth, he knew that he would have to be bolstered once more.

"Don't be concerned," Vanner said easily. "Everything is going to be fine. Just do exactly as I told you, and you'll never hear another word about this."

"I don't like it," Shanks said hoarsely. "It's an awful thing to ask anyone to do."

"Think of it as a performance," Vanner said. "Have you ever heard of psychodrama? No"—he smiled— "I'm sure you haven't. But surely you understand about traumatic experiences. Things happen to people, and when those things are the cause of great pain or fear or guilt they tend to suppress them, and bury them. You ought to know about burials, Mr. Shanks," Vanner's audience didn't laugh. "At any rate, we psychiatrists know that the only way to remove the bad effects of a suppressed memory is to re-create it. Do you see?"

"No," Shanks said, looking longingly at the sherry.

"Would you like a drink?" Vanner said, well aware from Shanks' effluvium that he had had several before his arrival. He poured him a glass.

Shanks bolted it like redeye and said: "You sure there won't be trouble?"

"The only 'trouble' would be yours, Mr. Shanks, if you didn't cooperate. Do you understand that?"

Shanks made a sorrowful search of his empty glass and nodded. Vanner took the glass from him and put it down carefully. "All right then," he said. "Come with me."

Vanner led Shanks into the front hallway as if by an invisible leash. The ex-undertaker looked up the long flight of stairs, fearfully.

"Just one more thing," Vanner said.

He went to the antlered coatrack in the hallway. On the marble-topped table beneath the hallway mirror, there was an object wrapped in brown paper and Scotch tape. He removed the wrappings and told Shanks: "Take this with you."

Sixteen

Dreams:

Clutching the chains of a garden swing in ecstatic terror, seeing her own legs swoop into the air, the tips of her black patent shoes like blackbirds flying in unison. Falling back to earth again, back into the clutches of gravity, rising again at the upswing, looking down and seeing beneath her the oblong depression in the ground, the piled-up dirt of gravity's grave . . .

Her father. A pink blur of a face under a visored

hat, the cold touch of buttons, buttons, up and down the length of him. Arms lifting her from the ground, the pretty golden leaves on his shoulders, touching them, trying to possess them. Her father laughing. Face against face, rough touch of beard and odd mixed smell of smoke and sweetness, feeling of safety and peace.

The clock. A tolling tower. Stairs rising toward its distant face. Climbing, out of breath. The bell tolling louder. Church bell. Bell. Knell. Hell. The devil pulling Cassandra by the tail. Howling. A man in a white coat, gauze mask over face, needle in hand. Point plunging into her rump. Cassandra whimpering, head on paws, eyes pleading, soft thump of tail on carpet . . .

She heard the thump twice, and opened her eyes.

So soft a sound in the stillness. Thump, pause, thump, pause. Thump paws? Gail thought. Thump tail? Cass the approximate sheepdog coming upstairs? No. Cass was dead, put to sleep. Still, the thump, pause, thump.

Silence.

She waited for sleep's gravity to draw her down again.

Waited, and heard the creak.

Her eyes went to the door.

Did the knob turn?

No matter.

The door was locked.

Dr. Vanner had latched it on his way out.

Let the knob turn.

But now the door was opening.

Against the diffused frame of light from the hallway, the black silhouette of the undertaker appeared in all its crooked angles and exaggerated length, one bony hand on the outside knob of her door, the other

clutching something to his chest; the man of wooden
boxes and excavated earth stepped inside her room
and into the soft glow of her night light, the low bulb
casting all its shadows upward, turning his eyes into
empty black sockets; the crooked body, faltering with
every step as if the carpet were some sort of treacher-
ous terrain, moved toward her. There was no other
sound in the room except his own frightened moans
because Gail's throat had turned into a solid column of
flesh that permitted neither sound nor breath to escape.

Then he stopped, midway between the door and her
bed, and his right hand emerged from underneath his
coat; something flashed metallically in the light as he
stiffened his arm and thrust forth the object he was
concealing, the spade that dug the grave that took the
boxes that held the bodies that death's own gravity
drew down into the everlasting night.

Seventeen

Struggling with him, shrieking at him, fingernails rak-
ing across his cheek, the bridge of his nose, the
bearded chin; but the undertaker had no beard. That
realization choked off her screams long enough for her
to hear Dr. Vanner's shouted commands. "Stop it,
Gail! For God's sake, stop it!"

Sobbing, she lifted her hands as if to ward off the
slap that would calm her hysteria. But Vanner simply

grasped her shoulders and pushed her firmly against the pillows.

"The undertaker!" she gasped. "He was here—he came for me! Just the way he did that night!"

"No," Vanner said. "No, Gail, nobody was here. You saw another phantom, another hallucination. Nothing more than that."

"It was him, I swear it! He came up the stairs, just the way he did the night my mother died. He came into my bedroom! How could I ever forget such a thing?"

"But you did," Vanner said wryly. "You buried that memory of your childhood completely. The fact that the undertaker entered your bedroom that night. You assumed he had come to take you next, Gail, to do the same thing to you that he did to your mother . . ."

"Yes. I thought he was coming for me! It was horrible!"

"You thought it was your turn in that wooden box. Your turn to be buried under the ground . . ."

Her sobs began again. "Oh, God, Joel, how could I not remember? It was the worst moment of my life!"

"It was your punishment," Vanner said. "That was what you believed when that man came into your room. Punishment for your evil thoughts, for your death-wish against your mother, the wish that had been fulfilled . . ."

"But I didn't dream it, Joel, I swear I didn't! Not then—not tonight!"

"No," Vanner said, stroking her hand. "You didn't dream his return that night, Gail, it was an actual event. The undertaker *did* come back. He came back to this house, and he mounted those stairs outside, and he opened your bedroom door and walked in. But he didn't come to get you. All he wanted was his brief-case."

"His what?"

"You see how mundane the source of our fears can be? Your friend the undertaker had left his briefcase in the house, and he came back to retrieve it that night. He came up to the second floor and opened up the door he believed led to your mother's bedroom. But he made an error. He opened your door instead—and that was the trigger that precipitated the mechanism of your illness. Not a dream."

"But it wasn't a dream tonight. It couldn't have been! I was awake, Joel! The man was as solid as you are!"

"You said that about Helen Malmquist."

She withdrew her hand from his. "But it's the truth," she whispered. "I saw him. He walked in exactly as he did that night. And—he had something with him."

"What?"

"Oh, God," she said, her voice distorted. "I don't want to tell you. I don't want to talk about it. You won't believe me!"

"I have to know the whole story, Gail. How can I help you if I don't know?"

"He had—a shovel. A small metal shovel, under his jacket. Maybe it was a spade; I'm not sure I know the difference." She looked at his expression and wailed: "Don't look at me like that, please! It's the truth! He had this spade under his coat, and he took it out and thrust it toward me as if to say—I'll bury you! I've come to bury you—with this!"

"Your door was locked," Vanner said gently. "You know that I locked it myself, with the key Mrs. Bellinger gave me."

"But he opened it! He was here!"

"No," Vanner said, infinitely sad. "The only thing that happened here tonight, Gail, was that something forced a monster out of the dark cellar of your sub-conscious. Why that happened, and what it indicates, may take a long time to determine. But the fact that it manifested itself as reality . . ." He paused and took her hand again. "That doesn't leave us with too many choices. The choice was limited long before this, but I didn't want to give up—I didn't want to admit that you had entered the hallucinatory stage of your illness . . ."

"It wasn't, it wasn't hallucination," she groaned, rolling her head back and forth on the dampened pillow. "I swear it was real, Joel, please believe me . . . help me . . ."

"I can't help you enough. Don't you see? You need total care. A complete immersion in the curative process. It's the only answer. You have to understand that."

"Oh, God, Joel! You don't mean—a hospital?"

"I'm not afraid of the old-fashioned word 'asylum.' There's nothing wrong with the word. 'Asylum' means a place of refuge, a place where you can escape the pressures that are destroying you. Because that's what will happen if you don't get help, if everything possible isn't done. Electro-shock therapy, therapeutic baths, drugs—"

"No! You wouldn't do that to me—I told you I couldn't bear that! I'd rather be dead!"

"But you *will* die if you don't get help. Your mind is dying. Disintegrating. The part of you that is *really* Gail Gunnerson is dissolving away . . . Is that what you want to happen?"

"No, please, no! You can't turn against me, too—I'll have no one left!"

"Gail, there's nothing more I can do for you. I'm as helpless as I was when . . . well, when poor Cassandra became sick. At least there was a choice there."

"A choice . . ."

"Your mother made one," Vanner said. "Didn't she?"

He reached into his pocket and removed the small white envelope. There were ten capsules left. He shook them carefully onto her night table. Two of them rolled up against the base of the porcelain balle-rina. He crumpled the envelope and dropped it into the wastebasket.

"This isn't like the other medication I gave you. These help you sleep, Gail. One will help you sleep for a night. Two for even longer. Four, or five, or six . . . Well." He looked at her eyes, and saw the slow development of awareness. When he was satisfied that she understood him completely, he turned and went out of the room.

As he went down the stairs, he thought about Shanks. The undertaker, startled by Gail's screams, had plunged down these stairs in such haste that he had tripped halfway and landed in an improbable tan-gle of arms and legs. Whimpering like a wounded ani-mal, he had hobbled out the front door; Vanner hoped that no late-night passers-by had witnessed the phe-nomenon of his exit from the Gunnerson house. But Vanner was only halfway down the stairs himself when he was stopped by the sound of Gail's voice.

"Joel! Please! Please, Joel!"

He turned and saw her on the landing, her night-dress twisted and disheveled, her hair in wild disarray, her face tear-streaked and grimy as a child's. He had a fleeting vision of the six-year-old Gail and her own terrified tears.

"Joel, I can't do it, I can't! There has to be some other way!"

"I have to leave now," Vanner said, his voice stiff with disapproval. "We'll make all the arrangements tomorrow. I'll have to speak to the Fiduciary Bank concerning the commitment proceedings. I don't know what time I'll return exactly."

"You mustn't do that!"

"My choices are as limited as yours."

She buried her face in her hands. Vanner sighed and came back to her. He put his arms around her shoulders and said: "Those capsules I left you are a very simple solution, Gail. I know it's wrong of me to offer it, but God knows I understand how you feel, even how your mother felt. All you'll know is a feeling of drowsiness and peace . . . I can promise you that, at least . . ."

But she was shaking her head. "I can't. I won't!"

"You prefer the asylum?"

"I just can't—don't you see? I want to live, Joel!"

"Do you think that's any sort of life?"

"Maybe I can get well again! Maybe now that I *know* about myself, I can get well!"

Harshly: "You call hallucinations getting well?"

"But you've made me *understand* myself! Maybe that's why I saw the undertaker again—because I was able to shake loose the memory at last! I was able to purge myself; isn't that what I had to do?" She clung to him with fierce strength. "You've helped me! You've helped me! I know I can be well now because of you . . . I don't want to die! I don't want to, Joel!"

He led her back toward the bedroom. "Go inside, Gail. Think about what it'll mean to live the rest of your life inside padded walls, to be treated like a wild animal . . ."

"I don't want to go back to that room!"

"You have to," he said angrily. "You know what will happen if you don't!"

"I'm going downstairs! I'm going to the kitchen. I'm going to eat something. I'm starved! Do you suppose that's all it was, just the lack of food? They say that mystics starve themselves to see vision . . ."

She reached out for the bannister, and Vanner snatched her hand from it.

"You idiot! Don't you see that I'm right?"

"Living is right, Joel, isn't it?" Isn't it?" She was trying to keep the tears from returning, but they came anyway. "Please let me go," she sobbed. "Please. I want to get away from that room . . . I want to see Mrs. Bellinger."

"Mrs. Bellinger is asleep, and you should be, too—"

"You're hurting my hand!"

"It's your last chance, Gail!"

"I won't go in there—I won't! Let go of me, Piers! Please let me go!"

He released her so abruptly that she almost toppled backward. She regained her balance, but she was assailed by another kind of vertigo. Suddenly, she was seeing the world through the wrong end of a telescope; the only way the past could be viewed. There was a stricken look on Vanner's face, the gray eyes rounded in consternation, the jaws slackened; it made him look younger; it made him look more like the boy he had been. "Why, you *are* Piers, aren't you?" Gail said wonderingly. "You're just like him," Gail said and whimpered when he thrust his hand over her face, the heel of his palm slamming into her mouth. Between his outspread fingers she saw the terrible red rage coloring his face from hairline to beard. Then his image blurred, and she was falling. She saw the grandfather clock, upside down. She cried out, but now the walls themselves were curving inward to enclose her, and she spoke his name again. *Piers!* she said, her voice faint and distant.

But Dr. Joel Vanner heard it and knew that he, too, had lost the privilege of choice.

He found no rope in the attic. That was fortunate, perhaps. Parallels were parallels. Cressie Gunnerson had used an electrical cord, and there was a lengthy extension in the parlor that he had tripped over more than once. He didn't like leaving the unconscious girl sprawled on the dusty floor; her cooperative blackout might end at any moment, and he hated to resort to the violence of a blow. That had been his worst moment with Helen; the necessity of clubbing her into unconsciousness in order to gain *her* cooperation in the suicide plan. Vanner shuddered at the memory of it; it had taken more out of him to deal that blow than it had taken to make the incisions in her wrists. It had something to do with eyes. He hated the fact that Helen was *looking* at him when she realized his intentions. But her eyes had been neatly closed by the simple act of slamming her temple against the side of the bathtub. The rest of the process was similar to working on the body of a mannequin. Gail was a mannequin now, for all intents and purposes. And her eyes were closed. Hopefully, they would remain that way until he could locate the cord and return to finish the night's labors. He hurried to the main floor, passing the door of Mrs. Bellinger's bedroom; he couldn't resist pausing for one moment to listen for the sound or lack of sound that would indicate sleep. He was gratified to learn that Mrs. Bellinger had a lusty snore. Then he went into the parlor, unplugged the cord from the floor lamp, and returned to the gallows site. Gail hadn't stirred. Once again, Vanner had cause to believe in Destiny's partisanship.

The noose he fashioned out of the brown rubbery cord wasn't perfect; a professional hangman would have sneered at it, but it would serve the purpose. He looped the other end over the center beam of the attic, employing the female portion of the plug as a throwing weight.

Then he looked about for a sturdy chair. There was a fine selection. He chose an antique but well-preserved Chippendale, testing its solidity by pushing down hard on the seat with both hands. It tested A-1.

When he went to lift Gail from the floor, he discovered that unconsciousness had its drawbacks. Unlike a mannequin, the dead weight of a human body was difficult to manage. He hadn't had much trouble carrying her up the stairs, but maneuvering her into the proper position wasn't easy. The smell of his own perspiration soon mingled with the musty odors of the attic.

Finally, he had the noose around her neck, and both of her bare feet on the Chippendale's fabric-covered seat. But when he removed his supporting arms, he found that her body sagged and almost slipped off the chair prematurely. He didn't want that; he had no desire to see the terrible first tug of the noose on the girl's delicate white neck. Or rather, he admitted wryly to himself, he was repulsed by the fear of her eyes opening suddenly, startling into consciousness by the pressure on her windpipe. Then he realized what the problem was: the Chippendale was a few inches too high off the ground; Gail's legs bent at the knees. But no matter. When the chair was no longer beneath her, she would clear the ground by at least ten inches, enough to do the job. He was still measuring the distance when the doorbell rang below. He had the unpleasant experience of feeling the perspiration on his body turn cold. He waited and listened, trusting that silence would drive the visitor away.

But the doorbell rang on, insistently, a sound deliberately amplified to carry to the far reaches of the large house, from front hallway to attic to bedroom

. . . Vanner swallowed and wondered if the housekeeper might yet be roused out of her mighty slumber by an even more powerful instinct to do her duty. He had to make his move quickly, and there was only one move possible. He kicked the front leg of the Chippendale, and the chair shot out from beneath Gail's suspended body; the brown cord grated against the beam overhead, and he heard the terrible crack of her neck breaking under the impact: it was a sound he wished he hadn't heard. As he hurried down the stairs to the ground floor, its echo stayed in his eardrums and affected his judgment. He should have determined who the caller was. Instead, he simply flung the door open and blinked vapidly at Steve Tyner.

"So you're still here?" he said. "Good, fine. I've got things to ask you, *Doctor,* lots of things."

"Let me pass," Vanner said hoarsely. "I can't talk to you now. I've got to get help."

"I thought we could have a talk, Doctor, about Viennese waltzes and, and Sigmund Freud, and a few other things—"

"Listen to me!" Vanner bellowed. "Gail has hanged herself!"

It had the stunning effect he anticipated.

"What did you say?"

"Gail committed suicide," Vanner said. "She hanged herself in the attic, just as her mother did. Oh, dear God," he said, with a totally genuine sob that could have been mistaken for anguish but was actually relief. "I tried to help her, I tried so hard, but I couldn't . . ."

Steve's shoulder struck him brutally as he thundered past him to the stairs. Vanner didn't mind the pain; he was barely conscious of it. He went outside, and the sight of his rented Plymouth delighted him, as if it had been a Christmas surprise. He climbed into the driver's seat and drove off, gunning the engine as he pulled away from the house, enjoying the sheer mechanical pleasure of feeling the wheels respond to his touch. It had been raining, but now the skies were clear, the air freshened and sweet, the roads sleek and black, polished for the occasion. He opened the window and let the breeze cool him. He was exulting in every sensation. When the incredible vision filled his rear-view mirror, his scream was contrapuntal to the sound of his tires on the macadam as the Plymouth plunged recklessly into the left lane. A station wagon struck its right front fender and sent it spinning in an eccentric circle; something or someone was ejected into the shrubbery along the highway, but miraculously the wagon was involved in no further collision, nor were the oncoming cars behind it. Then the Plymouth slammed into the low stone wall, its rear end rising into the air for one incredible moment of suspension, and then crashed downward again amid three explosions, two of them its rear tires, the third its gas tank; the last was accompanied by a lush globule of red and orange flame.

Eighteen

"Time changes everything," Baldridge said philosophically. "It changes things and it changes people."

"They both can go rotten inside," Steve said grimly. "Like Piers Swann. And like that beam in the attic, thank God. It must have cracked the second Gail's weight hit that cord. Yost says she's got nothing worse than a bruise on her throat."

"Yost? Is that the doctor's name?"

"Yes," Steve said, leaning back in the parlor chair and rubbing his bruised shoulder. "Nice old G.P. I like a nice old-fashioned G.P. with white hair."

"You still haven't told me why you came here to-night."

"Because of Vienna," Steve said wryly. "Because Vienna was cropping up too often. Swann lived there for the last five years before he and his papa went on that skiing trip in Zurich. And by a lovely coincidence, Dr. Joel Vanner was educated in Vienna. And then there was the restaurant."

"What restaurant?"

"The Hostario dell' Orso, in Rome. Very fine place —one of the best. Great food, nice music, strolling musicians playing Viennese waltzes. I guess Piers really got a taste for the stuff. Personally, I prefer Dizzy Gillespie. How's the coffee, Lieutenant? I made it myself. Believe it or not, the housekeeper is still asleep."

Baldridge grinned. "Almost as good as ours," he said.

The telephone rang. Baldridge knew the call was for him because he had asked Sergeant Shuster to call him from the hospital. Shuster was reliable. Baldridge listened carefully to his report, and then repeated it for Steve's benefit. Calvin Shanks would be a walking bandage for the next few weeks, but he would live. Aside from abrasions and contusions resulting for his hasty exit from the Plymouth, his only injury was a badly sprained ankle. And that, it seems, had resulted from a fall in the Gunnerson house.

"Swann put him up to it, all right," Baldridge said.

"Shanks said he was trying to re-create the fright that sent Miss Gunnerson into the booby hatch when she was a kid."

"But that wasn't his intention," Steve said. "Swann had nothing to gain by driving Gail crazy, and I'm sure he was too smart to think he could. All he hoped to do was make her *believe* she was coming off the spool, so she'd oblige him by killing herself. When that didn't work, it was do-it-yourself time. Listen, did Shanks say *why* he was in that car?"

"He couldn't walk when he left the house. He knew he couldn't make it to the subway, so he climbed into the back seat of the Plymouth and curled up like a wounded animal—which is pretty much what he was. Swann didn't know he was there until they were on the road, and when he saw him he must have over-reacted."

"Yes," Steve said. "I'd call it that."

Dr. Yost was coming downstairs. Steve got up so quickly that he knocked over his coffee cup; the brew was so thick it barely spilled. Yost wasn't wild about the idea of his patient being disturbed again, but Steve's plea was so eloquent that he relented.

When Steve entered the room, Gail was looking at the Pooh Bear lying across the foot of her bed. But then she gave Steve all her attention. Her mouth close to his ear, she said: "But isn't it strange, Steve? Isn't it all so strange?"

"What is?"

"That he helped me. That horrible man Piers helped me. I don't think I'll ever be afraid again. Not of doors or ghosts or goblins or lions or tigers."

"That's right," Steve said, surreptitiously lifting the stuffed bear by the paw and lowering him to the carpet.

How to stay healthy all the time.

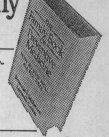

> "I can recommend this book for authoritative answers to questions that continually come up about health and how to live."—Harry J. Johnson, M.D., Chairman, Medical Board Director, Life Extension Institute.

Wouldn't it be wonderful if your whole family could stay healthy all the time?

It may now be possible, thanks to PREVENTIVE MEDICINE. This is the modern approach to health care. Its goal is to prevent illness before it even has a chance to strike!

A new book called THE FAMILY BOOK OF PREVENTIVE MEDICINE shows how you can take advantage of this preventive approach, and make it an everyday reality for yourself and your family. More than 700 pages long—and written in clear, simple language.

TELLS YOU ALL ABOUT THE LATEST MEDICAL ADVANCES

For example, the new knowledge of risk factors in disease is a vital tool of preventive medicine. With it, your doctor might pinpoint you as, say, a high heart attack risk *long before your heart actually gives you any trouble.* He could then prescribe certain changes in your diet and habits—perhaps very minor ones—that could remove the danger entirely. This would be preventive medicine at its ideal best! But even if a disease has already taken root, new diagnostic techniques can reveal its presence earlier than ever before. And, as a rule, the sooner a disease is discovered, the more easily it is cured.

SEND NO MONEY—10 DAYS' FREE EXAMINATION

Mail the coupon below, and THE FAMILY BOOK OF PREVENTIVE MEDICINE will be sent to you for free examination. Then, if you are not convinced that it can help you protect the health of your entire family, return it within 10 days and owe nothing. Otherwise, we will bill you for $12.95 plus mailing costs. At all bookstores, or write to Simon and Schuster, Dept. S-53, 630 Fifth Ave., New York, N.Y. 10020.